HIM NEXT DOOR

REBECCA CASTLE

PROLOGUE

THREE YEARS AGO

She's still in the car by the time I arrive at the scene of the crash.

I can already see her before I even make it close to the wreckage. I don't need superpower vision to make her out. I *know* it's her.

But I don't believe it.

I don't *want* to believe it.

She isn't moving. Her body is crushed between metal and glass. It's still *her*, though. The police have parked a car in front of the crash to try to block the view from bystanders, but it isn't enough to block me.

Even with all the blood and the lights and the shouting and the distance between us, I recognize her hair and her face in an instant. I've seen that face a thousand times before, but not like this.

I've seen that face laughing and smiling. I've seen that face be angry and sad. I've seen that face look up at me at the church altar on the day of our wedding with all the love in the world and say *I do.*

And now there's only one thought going through my head.

That's my wife.

I'm momentarily blinded by the spinning lights of the ambulance parked next to the crash. I raise my hand to my eyes. The crash is still fifty yards away or so, but I can clearly see everything.

Yep. That's her. She's really there.

"No, no, no."

The words escape my mouth.

And then I break into a sprint. Towards her.

I just need to see her. Hug her. See that face light up in a smile again. I need to make sure everything's alright.

But, deep down, I know it isn't.

I know nothing is going to be alright after this.

A police officer steps in my way, holding me back from reaching the crash.

"Sir! Sir!"

I know they're only doing their job, but I don't care. I want to reach her. I want to touch her. I want to know for real that she isn't breathing.

I want to be able to stop the inevitable.

She can't be dead.

I try to push past, but the policeman's arms are around me, pinning me in place. I struggle against him in vain.

"That's my wife," I pant, completely breathless. "That's my wife."

"I'm sorry, sir. You can't go any further."

My voice is quiet. Remote. Weak. "I should've been there for her. I should've helped her. I should've protected her. I'm her husband and I wasn't even there for her."

"I'm sorry, sir. I'm sorry."

"I just want to see her. Tell me, is she alright? Is she okay?"

I'm stumbling over my words. It's like my lips are numb. I don't even know if it's even me speaking. I'm just staring at all the twisted and broken metal that used to be my wife's car, not able to do anything else. The policeman holds my body.

I'm just staring at the body of the woman I hold close in bed every night.

But it's not her.

Not properly.

Even from here, I can see there's something different about the person lying in the crash. There's no spirit. No... *her* anymore. She isn't my wife, it's just a body now caught in a crushed vehicle.

A lifeless body.

Another statistic.

Another roadside fatality for the records.

The policeman holding me back turns to the ambulance, to the paramedic, looking for something to say.

I realize that everyone at the scene has stopped and is looking at me. Every. Single. Person. I must be making a hell of a lot of noise.

The paramedic frowns at the policeman, turns to me, and slowly shakes her head. I see the sadness written across her face.

It's all I need to know.

In the instant she shakes her head, all the energy drains out of me.

I collapse down onto the hot tarmac of the road. The police officer lets go of me.

And then the whole world comes crashing down. The

full realization of what's just happened hits me like a ton of bricks.

My wife is dead.

I cover my face with my hands and begin to cry.

* * *

I STAND on the edge of the cliff and breathe in. The crisp fresh air that flows up from the Pacific Ocean below fills my lungs. The beach below is just a speck of sand under my feet and the drop down is far. I am right at the very edge of this cliff, right in the danger zone of accidentally falling to my death, but I don't care.

Around me, there is no one else. Ahead is just the blue ocean that stretches on forever, and behind me there is just empty grass leading to a distant horizon. No cars. No living person for miles.

The sun is setting.

Everything is perfect. Beautiful.

Yeah, it's time.

I look down at the urn snuggled in my arms. I slowly remove the lid and delicately lift out a handful of ash.

In one strong go, I scatter the ash over the edge of the cliff. The air takes it, drifting the grains of dust over the ocean.

I continue to scatter the ash until the urn is empty.

I take a moment and watch it all disappear into the wind. I watch as the ash becomes one with the air. One with the coast.

She would like that.

And again, I take in a deep breath, I close my eyes, and I think I hear her voice echoing out to me.

I *know* I can hear her.

I stand there on the edge of the cliff and listen to her

telling me she loves me as her ashes dance in the air over the ocean.

And everything goes quiet. The grief leaves me. The pain of the last week dissolves as I listen to her voice calling to me. The images of that crash evaporate from my mind.

It's like she never left.

1

ELLIE

It all started when my husband ruined my life.

And all it took was four little words.

I want a divorce.

Four little words for my whole world to fall apart. Four little words for everything to come collapsing down around me. Four little words to ruin my sense of self and all the plans I had carefully laid down over years.

And, to top it off, the destruction of my life didn't happen in private either.

No.

My husband, in his infinite wisdom, decided to ruin my life in public. He thought it best to do it at a fancy restaurant, at precisely halfway through our meal.

On the date of our *wedding anniversary.*

I nearly choked on the Michelin-starred salmon when he decided to utter the words that would ruin my life. Those four little words were totally out of the blue for me. Totally unexpected.

"I want a divorce."

"Excuse me," I reply to the man I love sitting opposite me, struggling – in my state of sheer shock - to swallow the fish in my mouth and not allow it to regurgitate back onto the plate in front of me. "What did you just say?"

Have I just misheard him? Did he misspeak or...

Rich Turner - my husband of exactly one year *today* - leans forward across the table, his face stern. He's wearing a tailored suit. An expensive suit for an expensive man. I am dressed up equally glamorous as well. I picked out this dress just for tonight, and it didn't come cheap. I spent all day getting my hair done for this outing. I wanted to look beautiful for my husband. I wanted to feel sexy and strong. Happy for tonight's celebration of love.

I'd naively thought that this was going to be a nice anniversary dinner, and not a complete disintegration of our relationship. I never expected that I was shopping for a dress in which I was to receive the worst news of my life.

"Ellie, I don't want to stay in this marriage," my husband says. "I want a divorce."

Nope, I didn't mishear him. He really just said that. Twice.

I drop my knife and fork on the plate.

"A divorce?" I ask.

"Yes."

"A *divorce* divorce?"

"Yes.".

"You can't be serious. Is this some kind of sick joke?"

But I can see he's clearly not joking.

My husband rarely jokes.

And, right now, his lips have turned into the unmovable frown I know so well. It means only one thing.

This. Is. Serious.

"I just have to tell you straight out," he replies. "I want us to separate."

"But... it's our anniversary," I splutter. My mind is a mess, but at least I've managed to get the salmon down and not choke on it. "Our. Anniversary."

"I know, but I might as well say it now. I feel like this marriage is dull and unable to be saved," Rich continues bluntly. His words come thick and fast. I'm unable to process them as they flow from his lips. It all sounds like gibberish. Horrible, life-changing gibberish.

"Dull?"

"I think it would be best for us to part ways before things get out of control, and before we both start resenting each other. The earlier I tell you, the better it'll be for the both of us."

"But... on our anniversary?"

"Did you listen to what I said?"

"You're telling me this on our anniversary?"

He shrugs, like *I'm* being the unreasonable one here.

"Listen to me."

"You want to divorce me on our anniversary?"

I'm just repeating meaningless words now.

"Ellie?"

"What?"

"I don't love you."

"Oh."

"Sorry, but I had to say it, and now we have to deal with it, okay? Right now, we're sitting across from each other. There are no phones. No distractions. This is a perfect time to talk this through with you."

My husband is many things, but at least you can't say he's dishonest. He will tell you exactly what's wrong with you with all the subtlety of a sledgehammer. He will let you know exactly what's on his mind, no matter how devastating it is.

Or even inform you he wants a divorce when you're at your anniversary dinner, it seems.

And those four little words are definitely up there on the devastation metric.

And now I can add a whole new string of four words that have ruined my life.

I don't love you.

I'm at a loss for what to say, so I just repeat him like a parrot. "*Now's* the perfect time to talk this through?"

"We can go through this," he replies. "Calmly. Like adults. Or you can cause a scene, but I don't think that's the right thing to do, isn't it?"

"Why?" It's all I can whimper. My mind is blank. "Why are you saying this? Why do you want a divorce? Why don't you love me?"

My husband is unemotional. "I just don't feel... *me* anymore."

"What do you mean? You don't feel like *you?*"

"I don't feel like the person I thought I was."

"And what did you think you were?" I ask.

He shrugs. "Different."

"And this is to do with us?"

"It has everything to do with us," he replies. "I don't feel like me anymore."

"This has been going on for a year?"

"This has been going on ever since we got married."

"You've felt this way for the entire past year? You've never *loved* me?"

"Yes, Ellie. I thought this wouldn't come as a surprise to you."

"It's a *big* surprise, Rich. I don't understand," I stammer.

"I don't understand a single word you're saying. What's been wrong to drive you to this?"

"There's been a lot of issues."

"This is the first I've heard of any issues," I reply. "And this is because of our marriage?"

"Yes."

"You're not cheating?" I ask in a whisper.

Rich shakes his head. "No."

"Then what is it?"

"I told you. I'm just not... *feeling* this."

Okay, calm down, Ellie. Think this through. You're a smart, strong woman who's a manager at a top firm. This is merely another problem you have to solve. Work it out.

I can save this.

I reach across the table to take his hand. "And what can I do to help?"

"Nothing."

"There must be something I can do, Rich. Anything?"

"No, Ellie."

I go into full-on panic mode.

I really have to save this. Somehow.

"I can do anything, Rich. I can be whoever you want me to be. I can do whatever you want me to do. I'm prepared to work this out. You don't have to do what you're doing."

I am practically begging him. Pleading with him right here in this fancy restaurant. I'm too upset to even be embarrassed, though. I feel tears in my eyes. The eyes of everyone else in the restaurant are on me.

I'm getting emotional. And the last thing I am is an emotional person.

"You can have the apartment," he says like a robot going through a pre-programmed set of actions. No feeling at all. How very typical Rich; I bet he's thought through this all already. I bet he sat down and made a pros and cons list. You know, I used to find his organization skill kinda sexy, but now all I want to do is rip up his schedule into tiny little pieces and set it on fire. "I'll move out immediately. I've already made plans to live somewhere else until I get my own place."

"No, please. Rich. Don't leave me."

"It's too late. My mind's made up."

I grip his hand tighter, but he yanks it away from my grasp.

"What about work?" I ask. "What about us two?"

Rich is the CEO of the marketing company I work for. I'm one of his top managers. That's where we met, four years ago. A storybook work romance that blossomed into marriage. A *perfect* marriage, everyone told us.

And now it's the first anniversary of our wedding.

And now he's asking me for a divorce.

The man stands up from the table and pats down his jacket.

"I'm sorry, Ellie," he says. "I just can't do this anymore. I simply don't love you."

He's going to leave? Now?

"Please, Rich." Tears stream down my face. My makeup must look grotesque, all blotched and running over my cheeks, but I don't care. All I want – all I *need* – is for him to stay. "We can work this out. Please, Rich. Please. I can make you love me."

So pathetic, Ellie. You really think this is going to work?

But my husband ignores my pleading. Instead, he straightens his tie, turns, and walks straight out of the restaurant.

And I just sit there, looking down at my half-eaten piece of salmon. My whole world fallen apart.

I want a divorce.

I don't love you.

2

ELLIE

"HE SAID *WHAT* TO YOU?" Toni asks, her mouth dropping.

"He said he wanted a divorce," I reply, taking a sip of the Manhattan. "Oh, and he also threw in that he's never loved me as well, for good measure."

We're sitting in a cool bar downtown. It's Tuesday night, and the place is very quiet. It was Toni's suggestion that we meet up here. I haven't left home in days, so I really needed the excuse to get out of my pajamas.

I'm already tipsy and I'm only two drinks in. God, I'm such a lightweight. Perhaps that comes from not being a big drinker. I don't tend to like the feeling of getting all intoxicated and loose with alcohol. I'm usually the disciplined one of my group of friends, but today's not one of those days for me to hold back. Today's the kind of day for me to get seriously – and I really mean *seriously* – drunk.

"Just like that?" Toni asks, mouth still agape. "He just straight-up said he wanted a divorce and that he never loved you?"

"Yep," I say.

"He said that to you in the middle of your anniversary dinner?"

"Yep."

My friend leans back in her chair and closes her mouth, shaking her head in disbelief.

"Jesus."

"Yeah," I reply with a long sigh. "Exactly. *Jesus*."

"So, that's it?" Toni asks. "He's out of your life permanently?"

"Well, I haven't seen him since that anniversary dinner, so I guess that's it. He's gone. *Poof*. No contact."

"At all? Nothing?"

I take another sip of the Manhattan. "Not a single word."

Toni exhales deeply. "You know, he doesn't mention you at work."

I raise an eyebrow. "He hasn't said anything?" I ask.

"Nope."

"Wow."

Toni is another manager at the same marketing company. We work on the same floor and have been for the last few years. Like me, Rich is also her boss. She's a good friend of mine and has been since we first met. We've been in lots of scrapes together, but even Toni's never seen me like this.

She's never seen me falling into pieces. She's never seen the girl who's known for being so put together pulling apart at the seams.

"It's like nothing's happened," Toni replies. "He walks around the office like everything's completely normal. It's only because you haven't been there for the last few days and for the fact Rich has taken off his wedding ring that anyone suspects something's up."

"He's already taken off his ring?"

"Yep."

"Great, so it only takes him a couple of hours to get over it and yet I'm still stuck in self-pity three days on. It's like he's twisting the dagger in further."

"It sucks."

"Yep," I reply, taking yet another sip of the drink to numb the heartache. "It really does suck."

"What are you going to do now?" Toni asks, eyeing me cautiously, like I'm an emotional ticking bomb about to go off.

"I'm going to do what I've done since that dinner. I am going to sit around my apartment doing absolutely nothing."

"Not nothing, surely? Not you, Ellie. I can't imagine you sitting on your ass all day doing nothing."

I shrug. "What else is there for me to do? Everything in my life is *screwed*."

"It's not all screwed."

I've allowed myself the last few days to wallow in self-pity. I've always been a go-getter, I've always been the girl to repress the stress and pressure of the moment and just get on with the job at hand, but yet what Rich has done has completely and utterly thrown my life off course. It's like I'm lost at sea and I can't see land. I'm adrift in my own self-imposed selfish misery.

"I really didn't think it would turn out like this," I say. "Getting engaged was amazing. The wedding was perfect. I thought everything was going perfectly until this news hit. *Boom.* Now it's like there's no light at the end of the tunnel and I'm in darkness."

It's true. My routine, usually a well-oiled structured schedule, has been plunged into chaos since Rich's bombshell. I am usually so organized. So planned. Now it's all gone to shit.

I even planned for when I fell in love. I had a checklist – a proper physical checklist - for what I wanted, for what I *needed*, in a man, and Rich ticked all the right boxes. Some would even say our falling in love was purely strategic on my end. Conveniently falling in love with the CEO of the company I work at can sound pretty soulless to most people. But, hey, it's not exactly the *only* reason we fell in love.

And there are plenty of worse men to fall in love with than a rich businessman.

We've had a great few years together. We fit each other so well. Two high-flying conscientious people powering through the business world. We had our secretary's numbers on speed-dial, scheduling in dates into each other's diaries. Our dates consisted of big things that we designed around our busy lifestyles. Marathons together. Expensive restaurants. Theatre shows. We were the epitome of the upper-class Chicago couple. Cultured, physically fit, and smashing business goals.

And I tried, I really tried to be the perfect wife. I did everything for him. I was always available. I was always deferential. I always followed his plans. I read relationship guidebooks. I researched. I looked up crappy online articles on how to please your man in the bedroom. I improved myself for him. I made myself into the model of a perfect wife.

I just wanted him to love me because, despite my emotionless exterior, I really do love him.

Is it wrong for a gal to just seek a bit of romance in her life? To feel like she deserves a little bit of love?

And now that he's been taken away from me, I don't know what to do. I really am lost.

And you want to know the craziest thing?

If he called me up right now, I would go straight back to him.

Pathetic, I know.

But underneath my cold demeanor, underneath my routines and fitness regimen and diet, I'm still just a girl in love with a boy.

"It's so unlike you to be like this, Ellie," Toni says softly.

Before I can reply, our server appears at our side. He clasps his hands together. "Anything else I can get for you?"

Toni shakes her head. "We're fine, just the check please."

The waiter begins to turn away, but I cut him off.

"Actually, I'll have another Manhattan. And a bowl of nachos as well, please."

The waiter nods and leaves. I turn back to Toni. She's staring at me, gob smacked. Even more so than when I told her Rich wants a divorce.

"You're ordering more drinks?" she asks. "And... *nachos?*"

"I'm hungry. And thirsty."

"You're an imposter. Who are you and what have you done with Ellie Duke?"

"It's still me," I reply. "Just heartbroken."

More than just heartbroken, I've resorted to eating tubs of ice cream and watching sappy British rom-coms on my couch.

I *never* do that.

"I mean, I haven't even seen you at the gym the last few days, Ellie. You love the treadmill. It's crazy not to see you sprinting on that thing when I look up from the bike."

Like everything else in my life, my workout routine is scheduled down to the most minute detail. I run exactly four miles every day, do a timed routine I've paid a personal trainer very handsomely to compile, and I do an intense spin class every Tuesday and Thursday night. Everything in my week is precisely laid out. I have apps on my phone for every part of my fitness journey. I even count each and every individual calorie that passes my lips.

But not in the last few days.

"I'm just taking things slow," I say, shrugging.

"And there's no problem with that," Toni replies. "No problem at all. Maybe it is time to reevaluate your life. Breakups are a perfect trigger for that. Maybe you should see someone else. Go on a date. Get drunk and fuck the brains out of some random hot dumb model. Take a vacation somewhere and just process all this."

"No," I say. "I need to stop moaning and get back into things. I don't have time to wallow and get emotional, I've had three days of it and it's time to stop. Right after these nachos."

Toni leans forward in her chair and pats my arm tenderly.

"I've known you for more than two years, Ellie, and I've never seen you stop for a moment. You're like a shark. They always have to keep moving or they die. That's you to a *T*."

"I like that analogy."

"But maybe now you should change... *environments* for a bit," Toni continues. "Slow down for a moment. Don't be a shark for once in your life."

I scoff. "Nope. I never go on vacation."

"I know you don't, but maybe now you should. You should find something to do that's not your normal routine, something to occupy your time for a bit, something not related to marketing."

I scoff. "Like what, Toni? I'm not about to take up pottery or grow a garden."

"A little get-away, that's all."

"I just need to stop feeling sorry for myself and get back to work," I reply, repeating myself. "Three days away from it is already killing me. Like you said, I'm a shark. I can't stop."

"You do know *he's* going to be there, don't you?"

That makes me pause.

She's right. Rich is my boss. He will be all over the office when I go back to work. Meetings. Conferences. In the hall-ways. There'll be no way to avoid him or my heartbreak. It will take some immense willpower to go through that every day seeing his face. Hearing his voice. Willpower I know I don't have.

"Yeah, he will be at work, and I'll just have to deal with that as it comes."

"But what I'm saying is that you don't have to. Go on vacation, Ellie. Get out of here."

Ugh. Maybe she's right.

But what kind of vacation can I do? I'm certainly not the type to just laze around a sunny pool in the Mediter-ranean for two weeks. Knowing me, I'll probably end up hiking Everest or something.

My thoughts are broken by the return of our server with my drink and the nachos. I immediately dig in. Toni watches me and I feel like a greedy slug.

"You can't eat your emotions and then expect to go back to work all fine a few days later," she says. "You need to process this. Go on a vacation, Ellie. It's not a suggestion. I'm prescribing it to you."

"We'll see," I say, biting down on a crunchy tortilla chip.

In my language, that means *no*.

And Toni knows that.

"It'll be good for you," she says. "Please go. Please heal."

"Sure."

I give her a faint smile but I'm no longer thinking about work, or vacations, or Rich, or finding some new hobby.

I'm just thinking about that tub of choc mint ice cream currently sitting in my freezer that's got my name on it. I'll get through that and *then* I'll think about my future.

3

ELLIE

Julia Roberts is about to tell Hugh Grant on my TV that she's planning to stay in Britain *indefinitely* when my phone rings. I quickly pause *Notting Hill*, blow my nose into a tissue, wipe the tears from my eyes with my fingers, and answer the phone.

MOM flashes across the screen as I swipe. I sigh at the name.

Maybe I shouldn't be talking to her when I'm in such an emotionally vulnerable state.

"Hi, Mom."

"Sweetheart, how are you?"

"Fine."

"You're not still moping around in your empty apartment, are you?"

I look around me at the discarded tub of ice cream, all eaten, and at the pile of tissues lying in a pile on top of the coffee table that I've used to weep in. And not all because of the emotional effects of watching my third Hugh Grant rom-com today.

I'm curled up on my couch, practically in the fetal position, and I am feeling very sorry for myself. The only time I've moved today was stumbling from the living room to the fridge.

"I'm okay, Mom."

"Hm. I know that tone of voice. You really are not okay, Ellie."

Here we go.

In the last few days since Rich asked for a divorce, Mom has called me over thirty times. My phone is full of notifications from her. When I was properly married and living my normal life, my mother and I would barely speak once a week, but she can somehow sense when I'm vulnerable. And she isn't now going to let up an opportunity to coddle her only daughter, especially when said daughter is usually such an emotionless machine. Call it mother's instinct, I call it strangulation.

She's loving being the person I have to rely on. A proper Nurse Nightingale.

But, for once in my life, I do need a sympathetic ear. I'm usually so strong, so heartless. I've always been coldly business-minded.

But right now, I just need someone to talk to, and Mom has been all too eager to rise to the occasion.

"I am *fine*, Mom."

"Should I come over?"

"What? Fly all the way here from New York? Don't be ridiculous."

"Hm." She's unconvinced. Mom always liked a bit of drama, and I do too. She must be where I get it from. "I know you're not okay, Ellie."

I shouldn't be so hard on her. Mom also gave me her

best traits. Hard work. Dedication. She drilled those into me from a young age, and I am so thankful for that. There's no way I would've risen so far up in the corporate world so quickly if it wasn't for the work ethic my single-parent mother instilled in me. I'm only twenty-seven and I am already in charge of people twice as old as me. All thanks to Mom. So, yeah, maybe I shouldn't be so cruel about her.

Mom is great, but sometimes she does offer up the most insane solutions to problems, especially when it comes to matters of the heart. I will never forget the time, when I was a teenager suffering from my first ever break-up, when Mom decided it would be best to invite my ex to my birthday party as a surprise for me. To *resolve our differences*, as she put it. Well, that turned out to be a very predictable disaster, to say the least. She couldn't understand why bringing my ex to my birthday party less than a week after I broke up with him might *not* be the wisest move she could make. She still doesn't see anything wrong with that, even now.

"I'll get through this, Mom," I reply down the phone. I look up at my TV screen. Hugh Grant's face is frozen in that cute self-deprecating smile of his. I wish I was living in his fantasy Richard Curtis London and not in miserable real-life Chicago.

"Well, I'm always here if you need me," Mom says.

"Right."

"Anyway, I've been going through your uncle's things. You remember James?"

My ears pick up. "Oh?"

Mom's brother, James, passed away nearly a year ago. We weren't close. Not married and with no children, he practically left everything to Mom. He wasn't an exceptionally wealthy man or anything, and it wasn't like there were any major loose ends to tie up after he passed, so hearing that Mom's been through his things again is very unusual.

"I was just having a snoop through his records," Mom says.

"I thought you had that all sorted out," I reply.

"You know me, I was just double-checking we didn't miss anything after the funeral."

"Okay?"

"And guess what I found?"

"What?"

I can hear her voice bristling with excitement. She loves dropping some gossip and, judging from her voice, this one clearly seems to be *extra* juicy.

"He has, in his possession, a house."

"A house?"

"Oh, yes."

"A full house? How did you and the lawyers miss that?"

"Well, it isn't any ordinary house this one."

"No?"

"It's a *beach* house."

"Beach? Like next to the ocean?"

"What other kind of beach house could I be talking about, Ellie? Yes, he owns a beach house next to an ocean. It's all the way in some small town in California. Hang on, let me see what the name is." I hear her rustling through some paper.

"James certainly kept that hidden," I say. "I don't remember him living in California."

"He sure did keep it all hidden away," Mom replies. "And, yes, he never lived in California. Ah, here it is. The beach house is located in a town called Blue Haven. Have you heard of it?"

Doesn't ring a bell.

"No?"

"I guess you wouldn't. Apparently, it's a small place."

"And what are you going to do with this beach house in

this town called Blue Haven?" I ask, searching the empty ice-cream tub in front of me with my spoon, trying to find any last morsels.

"Sell it, of course. The lawyer I spoke to today came back with some records and it seems like it needs a lot of work done to it."

"You mean renovation?"

"Precisely. But I don't have the money to hire somebody for that. Plus, the whole thing will take weeks at least, most likely *months*. I don't want that kind of stress hanging over my head for nothing. No. I'll just sell it, I think."

I wasn't that interested in this whole beach house thing, but now, as Mom talks through the details of it, I hear Toni's words in my head.

You should find something to do. Something to occupy your time for a bit. Something not related to marketing.

And now I'm starting to get an idea.

Damn. This is exactly what my friend was talking about. A house to renovate.

A little get-away, that's all.

This beach house *is* in California. The opposite side of the country to cold Chicago, and somewhere hot at that.

It's on the opposite side of the country to Rich.

Go on vacation, Ellie. Get out of here.

Maybe this is exactly what I need right now. Get out of this funk I'm in. Reignite my life. Surely anything's better than sitting around eating junk food and watching nineties British rom-coms.

"You know what? I'll do it, Mom."

"You'll do what?"

I realize I've just been having a full-on conversation in my head that Mom hasn't been privy to.

"I'll renovate the place. I'll move in and work on it."

Argh, this is so spontaneous, and nothing like me.

But I'm actually certain about this. Maybe all the ice cream has gone to my brain and I've become insane, but as every second passes, it actually sounds more and more like a great idea.

"Really?" Mom asks. I hear the uncertainty in her voice. But I've not been surer of something for a long time.

I guess I'm going to California.

"Send me the papers for the beach house in an email. I'll sort it out. I'm going to do this."

4

ELLIE

I KEEP QUICKLY GLANCING down at the phone and back up to the road as I cautiously drive down it. The flashing dot on my phone screen tells me I should be *here*, but I don't think I am. It seems like I'm in the middle of nowhere. The road is empty, surrounded by trees. I can't see past the dense foliage.

Yep, literally in the middle of nothing.

I grip the steering wheel and cautiously turn the car around the bend, still checking the map on my phone to see if I am even remotely heading in the right direction.

This should be it. I hope I'm not lost.

It's only when I fully turn the corner and the trees part way to a view of paradise that I realize I've made it. The white sand of the beach greets me in the distance. I can see the blue of the Pacific Ocean. The road runs out at the front of a ramshackle building that rises up in front of me.

This must be it. This must be the beach house.

It really is a mess of a building. It appears that Uncle

James must have last visited this place in the nineteenth century. The photo Mom sent me of the place made it seem very different from the ruin it's turned out to be. The photo must've been taken years ago. It's way worse now. Worse than I expected. Nature has slowly overtaken the beach house. Green snaky vines latch on the outside walls. The wood paneling looks moldy and crumbling apart. It's going to have to take a lot of work to get this thing back into shape.

Is this where I'm supposed to live for the next few months? Maybe I was too hasty in agreeing to fix this place up.

It looks like an impossible job. I'm probably gonna need to hire some local help.

I park the car in front of the main door. I fish around in my bag for the house keys Mom sent me in the post. I've just spent the last two hours driving here to Blue Haven in this rental car from the nearest airport, and I am *exhausted*.

I glance back up at the ruin of a building.

I gulp.

I'm to sleep here? A bit different from my skyscraper apartment in Chicago.

I take a moment to sit in the car outside the place, letting myself breathe.

It now all suddenly feels very real and not just some crazy idea I had in my apartment.

"Alright, time to check this place out," I eventually say to myself, stretching my arms.

No time to hang around.

I get out of the car and walk purposely towards the front door.

But I don't need the keys, though. The front door to the beach house is already open.

Oh?

I gently push past the door and step inside. The floorboards creak under my weight. I glance around the living room.

Clearly, no one's lived here for ages. It's like a ghost house stuck in the seventies, and it obviously hasn't been redecorated since then.

But at the moment, I'm not too worried about the interior décor; I'm more worried about the strange sounds I'm hearing. Sounds that shouldn't be coming from inside an empty house.

Running water. Metal on metal. Clanging and banging.

Someone is in here.

What can this be?

I follow the sound around the corner from the living room. It's coming from the kitchen.

I step inside.

And then I see what's making such a racket.

In the kitchen, I'm greeted by an ass. An ass in tight shorts.

A *man's* ass.

He's bending down below the sink. I can't see his top half as he's deep inside amongst the piping.

And he's making a lot of sounds. He's doing something to the sink.

Who is this?

I grip the keys between my closed fingers as a weapon and I clear my throat.

"Excuse me?"

The sounds stop. The ass freezes.

Slowly, the man pulls himself out from under the sink. I ready myself if I need to make a run for it.

And then I see him. Properly.

He's not what I'm expecting at all. He's not some dirty mechanic or anything remotely like that.

Instead, he is gorgeous.

Short dark brown hair. A hint of stubble. And a straight jawline.

His face is perfectly structured.

But it's his body I'm looking at most. He isn't wearing a shirt. His muscles are on full display. Firm strong muscles. This guy either works out or he's lifting heavy things all day long. My eyes drift down to his six-pack, and to the shapely V that tantalizingly runs down into his shorts.

He looks me up and down, crouching down by the sink, and gives me a smile full of white teeth.

"Hello," he says.

Definitely not some grunting out-of-shape middle-aged handyman at all.

He must be around my age, or maybe one or two years older.

But no matter how much of a man-candy he is, I'm not prepared to let him off the hook.

"What are you doing?" I ask, tension building in my throat.

I am not ready to face some stranger standing in the middle of my property. I've only just got here.

His movements are slow. Relaxed. Unhurried, he takes his time to gesture at the floor around our feet.

"Fixing the pipes. It's been flooding."

And that's when I realize I'm practically standing in a puddle of water. It isn't too deep, but it is noticeable. So, this random guy is telling the truth. The pipes must've burst or something.

"Right."

I back away into the doorway, lifting my shoes away from the water in disgust.

"Well, it's fixed now," the strange man replies, pointing back to the sink. "Had to screw around inside, but I think I've solved it."

"Okay."

The less I talk to this weird dude, the better.

He chuckles. "Okay? Maybe a *thanks* might be more suitable."

"I'm not going to thank you," I reply. "You broke in. You need to leave. Right now. You're trespassing."

"I live next door," he explains. "I couldn't help but notice it was flooding when I walked past. I can't have this place falling apart. It's dangerous for me and my dog. And besides, I didn't break in. The door was open. That door is *always* open, so all I had to do was walk on in. No one lives here."

"Someone is living here now."

"Really?"

"I own the place."

He scoffs. "No one's owned this place for years."

"Well, I have a contract that says my family owns this place."

"Great, so now I know who to charge for my labor."

Now it's my turn to scoff. "No way am I allowing an intruder to ask me for payment."

The man shakes his head and stands up. He has no shoes on. The only thing he's wearing is those tight shorts.

"I've been living next door for ages," he says, pointing out the kitchen window at another house only a hundred yards or so down the beach. The *only* other house on the beach. "And I've never seen the owner here."

"This house belonged to my uncle. It's passed onto my mom, and now it's passed onto me. I'm going to fix it up and sell it."

He looks up at the ceiling that's falling apart and then back down at the leaked water lapping at our toes.

"Good luck with that," he replies.

Ugh. He's so annoying.

"Okay."

I want this random conversation to end.

"You'll need to install air-con pretty quickly, or at least get a fan," he says.

"Why?"

"It's going to be pretty hot at night. Unbearably hot. You won't be able to sleep if you're planning on staying here."

I roll my eyes. I've had enough of him. "Thanks for the tip. Maybe you should leave now."

"You could at least thank me."

"For what, exactly? For breaking in?"

"For fixing your sink."

"Why? I didn't ask you to do that."

"Because it's a nice thing to do, especially if we're gonna be neighbors."

"Well... thanks, I guess."

He smiles. Again. "That's better. See you around."

"Bye."

He walks past me to leave, but as he gets to the front door, he turns around. "I'm Declan, by the way. Declan Page. But everyone calls me Dec."

"Ellie Duke," I begrudgingly reply.

"It was nice to meet you, neighbor."

"Sure. Nice to meet you."

And then he's gone. Out the door.

I sigh, watching him stroll across the sand to his house opposite. He does have an *amazing* body. I observe his thick biceps and his nicely carved ass as he walks away. It's a mighty fine ass.

But the man's cocky. He really thought he had me all flustered. And yeah, he kinda did.

Great. I've got a beach bum for a neighbor.

Declan Page. Dec to everyone.

Whatever.

And he lives so close. I can practically see into his living room from my kitchen window. His place looks very similar to mine. It's the same layout and structure. Except mine is crumbling around me and his is in pristine condition. He clearly spends a lot of time fixing his place up.

But say what you want about the house, at least it has a view. A pretty damn good one at that. If I do manage to do this place up, I just know it'll fetch a pretty price on the housing market. The beach is empty other than the two houses. A pristine stretch of white sand leading into the clear blue ocean. Most would call this a little slice of heaven.

If only you shared heaven with some weirdo man who feels like he can break in anywhere he likes topless.

I tut at myself for still thinking about my new neighbor and turn away from the window.

I didn't come out here to think about men. Shirt or no shirt.

It's time for me to focus on myself now. It's time to get my life in order. I've lived on a diet of ice cream and pizza for the last week, and now I've gotta purge it from my system.

I feel so groggy after the flight and the long car journey here. I know what I'll do.

I'll go for a run.

5

DEC

I RIDE down the wave on my surfboard; the wind rushing through my hair. The salt air fills my nose as I skim across the surface of the ocean. I crouch, feeling the fiberglass board under me skip across the water as I maintain my balance.

The sun is up. The swell is good. It's a beautiful day.

Perfect.

I look up from the blue water towards the sand. The two beach houses stand in front of me. Mine and Ellie's. One a perfectly normal house, the other a crumbling ruin.

I shake my head and continue surfing.

I didn't expect anyone to barge in on me as I fixed the pipes in the abandoned house this afternoon. As I told the woman who charged in so aggressively, I have never seen the owner of the house in all my years of living opposite it.

The last thing I expected when I crouched down under the sink today was for *her* to come storming in with her demanding tone and accusations about me breaking in.

But I must say, it was a pretty funny interaction.

It's been a long time since someone spoke to me like that. It's been a long time since I've seen a stranger come into this small town.

And she says she's going to redo the place?

Yeah. Like I told her, good luck with that.

The abandoned beach house has been a running joke in Blue Haven for a very long time. No one wants to touch it with a ten-yard pole.

Until this Ellie Duke came along.

I twist the surfboard so that I shoot to the top of the wave and look back at the shore.

And there she is. I spot the woman in question. She's running across the beach. I can't make it out from this far, but it seems like she's wearing some kind of spandex. Some kind of fancy running uniform.

Why not just shorts and a shirt?

It isn't a fashion parade. No one's out here that can see you, Ellie Duke. Except me.

It's like she's at some big sporting event and not just out on a jog on the beach.

I shake my head and smile.

What is she really doing here?

She's cute, but she's clearly a city girl. If I couldn't tell with her spandex, I can just tell from her general attitude. I bet she's never stayed in a small town before. I bet she's never tried to fix up a crumbling shack, let alone pick up a hammer in all her busy city life. She's a tourist, nothing more. Way out of her depth.

But she *is* cute. Slim, with brown eyes that match the color of her wavy hair. She's pretty, *beautiful* even, if only she learned to smile instead of frown all the time. Even when she's running, she looks like she's a judge about to deliver a guilty verdict. I like the snarky attitude she dished out to me in her kitchen earlier. She has balls. I give her that, even if she's arrogant, stuck-up, and a little bit condescending.

But I'm not interested. I have my own shit to deal with. Besides, I've sworn myself off women, and have for a very long time. There was only ever one for me, and now she's gone.

I continue riding the wave with the skill of a pro surfer, watching my strange new neighbor as she jogs at a fast pace across the sand. She's good at running. She must work out a lot.

And then I spot Brandy sprinting towards her. My dog, a Labrador Retriever, can get *very* excited, especially when she meets a new person. She loves to sniff out new human smells.

And right now, she's latched onto Ellie.

Let's see how this pans out.

My dog bounds down the beach from my house towards the jogger, her tail waving furiously. She must've found a way out of the house while I've been surfing. She sprints all the way up to my new neighbor, her tongue hanging loosely from her mouth.

I watch Ellie as she stops and raises her hands in a panic as Brandy jumps up at her in excitement. It seems like Ellie's never owned a dog before; she doesn't know what to do or how to deal with one.

I laugh and spin my board around, heading back to shore.

I better sort this out.

I emerge from the waves, my hair wet on my face, and head over to Ellie. She's trying to cry out to my dog like she's a child to be disciplined.

"Stop, stop! Get down!"

Brandy thinks she's trying to play and therefore jumps

up on her even more eagerly.

I purse my lips together and let out a short loud whistle, immediately stopping Brandy and calling her back to me. She sits down by my side, panting. I readjust the surfboard held under my arm and give Ellie an apologetic look.

"We meet again," I say.

She isn't impressed.

"You need to train your dog," she says, panting nearly as much as Brandy. "She's a terror."

"Oh, Brandy? She's well-trained," I reply, turning to my dog. "Roll over."

She does so.

"Play dead."

She falls to the ground and lies still.

"Stand."

She gets on all fours.

"Bark."

Woof.

"Sit."

She does so without a pause.

I turn back to Ellie.

"See? Well-trained."

My neighbor shoots me an annoyed look. "Alright, you've made your point."

"It was pretty funny watching you try to handle her."

"There was nothing funny about it."

"Oh, come on. Loosen up."

She shoots me another deadly glare.

"Loosen up when an animal is attacking me?"

"You've never dealt with a dog before?" I ask.

"I'm not really an animal person," she says.

"I can see that," I reply. "Me? I love animals, especially dogs."

Ellie rolls her eyes. "The surfer dude and his dog. How very Californian."

"I'm a sucker for stereotypes. I'm guessing you're not from here. Whereabouts are you from, if you mind me asking?"

"Chicago."

I whistle. "Ah. The big smoke."

"You've ever been there?" she asks.

"I haven't even left this state."

"Maybe you should travel a bit."

I shrug. "I'm happy here with my dangerous jogger-eating dog."

"Right. Well, see you around, California."

She starts to walk back to her place.

Damn, she looks so hot in her tight spandex. She's sweaty. Wild. I could rush over and pick her up right here and fuck her on this beach.

My cock twitches under my pants.

I hope she didn't realize that I've been nursing an erection this entire time we've been talking.

Because I have.

"Hey, I can tell Brandy really likes you," I say.

Ellie stops and frowns. "She jumped up at me. I doubt that's *liking* me."

"Sure it is. She's not usually that open and playful with a completely new person, so it's pretty obvious she likes you."

"Okay, I'm going back inside now. Bye."

She turns to go, but I call out to her again before she gets too far away.

"Why are you here?"

She turns back around with a scowl. She doesn't like me constantly stopping her like this. Good. "To redo the house."

"No, why are you really here?" I ask.

There must be more to this woman and to her reasons for jetting out than just a vacation.

She doesn't answer. Instead, she shrugs and continues walking back to her place.

I think about calling out to her one more time, just in spite and to humor myself, but I hold back my tongue. Instead, I wait for her to disappear into the house before I head back to mine, calling Brandy to jog beside me on the way.

"What a strange woman, Brandy."

My dog *woofs*, I'm sure in agreement.

6

ELLIE

THE ACTUAL TOWN of Blue Haven isn't far away from the beach house, but it's still a massive pain to find. The map on my phone keeps cutting out thanks to the absolutely dreadful reception around here.

And I thought we live in a first-world country, yet technology doesn't work at all just because I'm close to a beach. Great.

I tut loudly at my phone as I navigate the rental car around the small coastal roads of Blue Haven, searching for a sign to point me in the right direction.

I'm also doubly annoyed at Declan "Dec" Page next door, and that dog of his. I am definitely *not* an animal person; my life back in Chicago was way too busy to even consider having a pet. Animals mean commitment. They mean chaos. They mean having to constantly change your schedule, and that is certainly not me. I find my enjoyment in action, in setting out tasks and completing them. I've never had a dog because that would mean taking time out of my diary to deal with them.

I simply don't understand people like Dec. Chilled people who can relax on a beach all day, surfing, with no schedule to speak of except for when they walk their dog and cook their dinner. I could never live like that. I need stress all the time in my life. I *thrive* off stress.

I could never see myself with a man like Dec Page.

But he is hot.

Alright, yeah, he was pretty damn gorgeous emerging from the surf all wet like that with the board tucked under his arm. Yeah, he knows how to flash his muscles. I can't lie; there was some part of me that went all soft and wet at the sight of him on the beach.

And yeah, it was kinda sexy how easily he had command over his dog. I can only imagine what a man with such alpha control like that would be like in the bedroom...

But getting all gooey over some beach bum is *not* me. I did not come all the way out here to find some hot dude to lose my heart to. I am here for one thing. Renovate that beach house.

Which is why I'm driving into Blue Haven.

I finally drive past a sign that indicates what turn-off I have to head down. I follow the road until the trees clear and the buildings of Blue Haven's main street appear into view.

Phew. Found it.

A small town is too generous a description for Blue Haven. It's just a scattering of one or two shops, a bar, and a post office. I feel like I'm living out in the wild west, if only you swap cowboys for surfers.

I drive up along the main street until I arrive at where I'm looking for.

Morgana's Hardware.

The only hardware store in town, or for at least the nearest fifty miles. I Googled that to double-check. This should be the place to get started on the home renovation project.

I park my car in the lot beside the store and step through the front door of the place, removing my sunglasses.

I've never been inside a hardware store before. I deal with numbers. Marketing. Phone calls. If I've ever needed something physical done to my apartment, there has always been an app to tap or a person to call.

But I'm determined to try my hand at this beach house. Maybe if I get the help of someone, then I can get a good handle on what to do.

Inside, Morgana's Hardware is just what I expect a small-town hardware store should look like. Rows of ropes and shovels and paint tins.

A bell rings when I step in, and a little boy jumps out from behind the counter. He must be no older than eleven. Crew cut black hair. He grins at me, then turns to the doorway leading into the back of the shop.

"Jennifer!" He calls in a singsong child voice. "Some-one's here."

"Tell them we're closing," comes the person from the back.

"It says on Google you're open till seven," I call out around the corner at this mysterious Jennifer.

The person out back doesn't reply. Instead, I hear foot-steps shuffling around the corner. A woman appears. Mid-thirties with dark blonde hair and a slight smile.

"Well, Google's wrong," she says, wiping her hands on her shirt. "I'm Jen Morgana, owner."

She offers out a greasy hand. She must've been working on something back there.

I'm a bit taken aback by the gesture. You would never come across a shop owner so friendly like this in the city.

Small town niceties, I guess.

I shake her hand, hiding my distaste at the grease. "Ellie Duke."

She points at the young boy. "That's Aaron. He's my neighbor's son. He helps me out in here."

"Hi, Aaron."

The boy continues to smile at me.

"So, what can I do for you, Ellie?"

"Well, I've actually got a pretty big task. I'm renovating a house and I'm looking for some help."

Jen raises an eyebrow. "You're new in town?"

"Just arrived today."

"What place are you renovating?"

"A beach house."

Jen's cheerful expression changes. Her smile drops. "The empty one down the road just outside of town?"

"Yeah, that one."

Jen whistles in astonishment. "No one's lived there for years."

"Yep, I know. I'm living there now while I do it up."

"You own it?"

"My family does. We guessed it'll be nicer if I did it up rather than just sell it, you know?"

"Well, that'll be a tough one to do up if the state of the inside is anything like the state of the outside."

"Exactly, and that's why I'm looking for some help. I'm willing to pay for someone's time and skill, if you are willing to help me."

"I would usually offer up my services, but for this one, you need an expert," Jen replies. She searches behind the shop counter for a pen and paper. She writes down a number, tears the strip off, and hands it to me. "Send him a message. He's the town's resident handyman. He practically does everything for everyone around here. He's the best in town. You won't find someone better. He should be able to fix up that place with you, although he'll definitely want payment for a project that big."

"I'm happy to pay," I reply.

"Good, because it's gonna be a big project."

"Yeah, tell me about it. Thanks, Jen."

"No problem, and if you're looking for any supplies, you know where to find me."

I give her a nod and head to the door outside, happy I've managed to grab the number. But before I leave the shop, I turn back to Jen and Aaron.

"It's my first day here, and I'm pretty hungry," I say. "I've tried Googling places to eat around here, but nothing pops up."

"I guess you use Google for everything, huh?" Jen asks me with a smirk.

"Well, yeah."

"Blue Haven is not really the most Google... *friendly* town," she replies. "We're too tiny for big tech to really notice us."

"Yeah, I've come to realize that."

"I would recommend the bar opposite. Well, I say *recommend*, but really, it's the only place you'll be served food around here. It's the only place I can recommend because there aren't any others."

"Oh, right. Thanks. Well, I guess I'm eating there tonight."

7

ELLIE

Blue Haven's bar is not exactly the pinnacle of fine dining.

I take a seat at a corner table and have a look around the place. A few regulars, drunk, sit at the bar. There's a group of middle-aged women sitting in the other corner gossiping. A few guys in construction overalls drinking beers lean against a wall. Just a lot of people here for post-work drinks.

There's a dart board. Pool table in the corner. The place stinks of dried Budweiser and salted peanuts.

A stereotypical small-town bar.

I would never frequent a dive bar like this back in Chicago. I'm more of a fancy rooftop bar gal myself. Prosecco and Rose, not beers and nuts.

Yep, I don't think any Michelin judges would be making a stop here.

But what should I expect in such a place? I roll my eyes at myself.

Stop being so effing arrogant, Ellie. You're not in Chicago anymore.

This is the kind of living I signed up for, and it sure as hell beats working in the same office as Rich. I need to shut up, take a chill pill, and soak in the small-town experience. I need to stop being so casually rude about everything here just because it's different.

You knew Blue Haven ain't gonna be like Milan. Time to get to know a different type of life.

I pull out my phone and the teared-off piece of paper Jen at the hardware store gave me, squinting to read the scribbled set of numbers on it. I input them into my phone and type out a message to this handyman that is supposedly the only person here that can help me. I delete and retype the message nearly a dozen times before I come up with something alright. If I'm to spend a lot of time with this handyman over the next few months, then first impressions count for everything.

Hi! I'm Ellie. Jen at Morgana's Hardware offered me your number. I'm planning on renovating the old beach house just outside town and was inquiring if you would kindly offer me a quote on your services? Thanks. Ellie.

Is it too formal? Too much like something a stuck-up marketing manager would write? I honestly don't know.

I take in a deep breath, take the plunge, and hit *send*.

The message flies off into the digital atmosphere and I sink into my seat.

Yeah, I'm gonna definitely need help with this beach house.

It was pretty foolish of me to think I could do it on my own, that I could read a few books and watch a YouTube video and suddenly become qualified to rebuild a house.

My stomach rumbles and I realize I haven't eaten since I landed.

I order at the bar. A cheeseburger and fries. Even though I should be jumping onto a better diet now, I think I might just stick to the safe option here. You can't really screw up a burger and fries, yeah? I don't want to spend next week in the thralls of food poisoning.

And there you go again, Ellie. Tearing into this town just because it's different from the luxury skyscrapers you're used to.

I need to purge myself of this unnecessary and cruel judgment. Maybe this sleepy coastal town will make me a hippy. Maybe it'll make me a Zen-like beach bum like Dec Page.

Yeah, that'll be the day.

I take my seat again and wait for my meal. My phone pings on the table.

A new message.

It's from the handyman.

Sure, Ellie. I'll come round tomorrow around five in the afternoon if that's okay with you?

I quickly send off a reply in the affirmative, then scroll through my social media.

My feed is full of high school friends getting married and work colleagues having kids. The usual stuff to see on a late-twenties Instagram feed.

Except it makes me stop and think. *I* should be posting happy photos right now under the caption of my own wedding's one-year anniversary. I should be boasting about my happy marriage on social media.

But I can't.

Stop thinking about him, Ellie. It'll only break your heart more.

In a desperate attempt to get my mind off my husband - my *ex*-husband - I check my emails.

That's a mistake. A big one.

I see pretty quickly that Rich has emailed me.

My body sinks when I see his name pop up in my Inbox. My heart is in my throat.

I know I shouldn't open it. I know that I should just delete the message and keep scrolling, but curiosity gets the better of me.

I click it and read the whole thing in one quick anxious go.

Ellie. It's been a week since I've last heard from you and I'm starting to get worried. Where are you, Ellie? I see you've put in a vacation request at work. I want you to know I've denied it. I gave you a few days off after the breakup to get yourself back into order, but now you've gone and completely disappeared. I need you back at work. You're our best manager. And I need to see you. I want to sort through everything, including the divorce papers I've had my lawyer draft up. I went to your apartment today, and you weren't in. Where have you gone to? Message me back as soon as possible.

I can't process it. The message is just... too much for me to handle right now. Rich is on another planet if he thinks he can control me. And he's denied my vacation request?

I did put in a request for a month. I have saved that much vacation time. I don't even know how long I'll be in Blue Haven for. As long as it takes to renovate this damn beach house, I guess.

However much I'm terrified of seeing Rich again, I don't want to lose my job. I'm not going to be here forever. I'll want to get back to Chicago at some point. I still want to slide back into my old life.

But not now. And why can't Rich see that? Why can't he grant me the time to recover?

My mind is totally fried. I need to distract myself else I

might go into a full-on breakdown in this bar and embarrass myself in front of all my new neighbors.

I came to Blue Haven to escape Rich, but now he is dominating my head.

I make my way to the bar and order a drink. Two drinks. A beer and a shot of whisky. It's time to get drunk.

8

DEC

DEREK'S SLUMPED up against the outside wall of the bar, his head bowed.

He's definitely in bad shape.

"You alright?" I ask him as I approach.

The man mumbles something incoherent at me.

"Had a bit too much to drink?" I ask, crouching down to look at his face. His eyes are closed and he's drooling saliva from his mouth.

I chuckle.

If any other person I know was in this state alone outside the bar, I would be alarmed, but not with Derek. He's the town drunk. I don't think I've ever seen him anywhere beyond the immediate radius of Blue Haven's bar, staggering around with a bottle in his hand. I've had to sort him out numerous times in the past.

"Right, let's deal with you," I say, looping my arm around his shoulders so I can hold on to him tight. All his weight falls on me. It's okay, I can deal with him. Derek is a much smaller man than I am and, at six-foot-one, I can do a decent amount of heavy lifting.

Pushing the door open, I pull Derek inside the bar. The place is crowded. After-work drinks seem to be in full swing.

I bring the drunk over to the side of the bar and whistle over Pete, the bartender.

"He's had a few too many," Pete comments when he sees Derek slouching over the bar counter. I grip the poor man by his shirt to stop him from rolling onto the ground.

"Yep, I reckon he has," I reply to the bartender. "He might need a glass of water."

Pete nods and fills one up, handing it to me. I press the glass against Derek's lips and slowly tilt its contents into his mouth. The man splutters, shocked at the cold liquid that isn't alcohol, but he still swallows. I smile at Pete.

"Well, at least he isn't unconscious," I say.

"Yep."

"Busy night?" I ask the bartender.

"Yeah, busy."

"Good."

"And how have you been, Dec?"

I shrug. "You know me, same old. As long as I have Brandy and my health, all's good in the world."

I'm a pretty private person. I've had enough bad experiences to know that gossip and rumors fly fast in a small place like Blue Haven, and I'd prefer to keep out of the limelight. I don't need everyone around town prying too much into my business. But even that sometimes can't be helped. I see the pity in people's eyes when they spot me. I know they can only see me as the lonely young widower.

"Maybe you should find yourself a girl, Dec."

"Yeah, when pigs can fly."

"You're a funny man."

I scoff. "Well, maybe stop laughing at me and get me a beer."

"On it, boss."

He flips open a bottle, sliding it towards me.

And then the most screeching noise explodes in the bar.

Pete and I cover our ears at the sound. It's pretty deafening. I turn to look at the source of the pain.

On the other side of the bar, someone is trying to sing into a microphone. *Sing* being a very loose definition of what they're doing. It's more like a high-pitched squawk.

"Don't. Stop. Believing."

Is this an attempt at karaoke?

Oh god. Make it stop.

I finally catch a glimpse of this sound perpetrator through the drunk cheering crowd. My jaw drops.

It's Ellie Duke.

My neighbor? The rude girl from out of town?

She's holding the microphone in one hand and a bottle of beer in the other, her feet swaying under her. She's incredibly drunk.

I laugh. She's funny. Maybe she isn't as stuck up as much as I first thought; she seems to know how to have a good time. I look around at the rest of the bar, who are all now staring at her. So, she isn't afraid to embarrass herself in front of everyone else? That's kinda cute.

She slurs through the rest of the song. My ears adjust to her particular brand of "singing" and I manage to watch the rest of her performance pain-free. It's just a lot of fun seeing the city girl with the stick up her ass let her hair down like this. I sit back on the barstool and take it all in, laughing.

Finished, Ellie does a wobbly bow before attempting to get off the stage. She doesn't make it far, though, before she trips over her own foot and falls, headfirst, onto the ground.

Pete and I rush forward to help her. No one else in the

bar does. They simply turn back to their drinks and conversation as if she was merely entertainment that's finished.

Ellie lies on the ground in front of the microphone, her hair scattered everywhere. I look at Pete and we slowly turn her over. I'm relieved to see there aren't any signs of blood, just a mumbling Ellie Duke being very drunk.

"She's unhurt," I say.

"She should go home," Pete adds.

"I agree. Like our friend at the bar, Ellie's had a bit too much to drink, I think."

"She's new in town," the bartender says. "I don't know where she lives or who to call."

"Don't worry, I'm her neighbor," I say. "I can take her home."

"You sure?"

"Yeah, she won't be the first drunk I've handled tonight."

It takes the bartender and me a moment to lift the girl up to her feet. Even though she is conscious, she refuses to stand. She's acting like a dead weight.

She's being so unhelpful that I have no choice but to carry her off the ground in my arms. She snuggles in against me as I slowly navigate my way out of the bar, giving Pete a wink on the way out.

I came out for one beer and now have my new neighbor lying in my arms.

I carry her all the way to my pickup truck across the street. She lies in my arms, limp. It's a struggle, but I finally manage to strap her into the front seat and begin to drive us home.

Ellie sits still for only a moment before she starts talking. Well, it's less than talking and more like a rambling string of words.

She eyes me up and down, giggling like a schoolchild.

"Oh, hello there, mister neighbor. You have a shirt on. That makes a very big change."

"Hello, Ellie. You okay? You had a bit of a nasty fall back there."

"Meh, nasty falls mean nothing to me. I'm pretty strong, you know."

"I bet you are, miss."

She tries to sit up to look out the window, but she slides back down the seat. "Where are we going?" she asks.

"You've had too much to drink for one night. I'm driving you home."

"But I am... I *was* having so much fun. Lots of singing."

She hiccups, and I laugh. "Yep, a lot of singing, Ellie. You've had a bit too much fun for one evening, and now it's time for bed."

"Ugh, you're no fun."

"I don't think I could keep up with you."

"No, you couldn't."

"It's time for bed now though, American Idol."

"Ugh. If you insist."

"We'll be home soon, then you can go to sleep."

There's a long pause. I'm too focused on getting us home safe that I don't take my eyes off the road. I think she's gone to sleep, but then she speaks again. Loudly.

"Do you know what my favorite flowers are?" Ellie asks.

"Flowers?"

"Yeah, do you know what my favorite flowers are?"

"No, I don't know what your favorite flowers are, Ellie."

She pokes a finger into my shoulder. "Chrysanthemum. Yellow chrysanthemum."

I laugh. "Good to know. I'll remember that."

"Do you remember what you said to me?"

"When?"

"This afternoon. Do you remember what you said to me?"

"What did I say to you?"

She is *so* drunk. Her head rolls from one side of the seat to the other.

"On the beach earlier today. This afternoon. You said... you *asked* me what I was really doing here."

"I did."

"And I didn't say anything."

"You didn't."

"Well, I'm going to tell you now, but I want you to keep it *hush-hush*, okay? I don't want sober Ellie finding out I told you my secrets."

"You don't have to tell me anything, Ellie," I say, turning around the corner out of Blue Haven's main street.

"I want to tell you why I'm here, though."

"Okay, sure."

"But don't tell sober me."

This is fun.

"My lips are sealed," I reply.

"So. My husband asked me for a divorce last week."

"What?"

"My husband asked for a divorce. Only last week. On my anniversary."

"You really don't have to tell me this if you don't want to, Ellie."

"Nope. I am. And you're gonna listen, alright?"

"Alright."

Ellie proceeds to tell me all about her life back in Chicago. Her time rising through the ranks at her marketing firm. Meeting her husband at the same workplace. Their life together. How happy she was. How she thought that it was going to be forever. And she tells me all about her divorce and all the heartbreak she's in.

"I just needed to get away, you know? Escape. Live a different life."

"You must be really upset, Ellie."

"I am, Dec. I really am. I've never been so sad in my entire life. My heart hurts."

"Well, the lifestyle here seems pretty different from your one in Chicago."

"Exactly. I thought I had forgotten all about Rich, but then he emailed me at the bar tonight, and then, because of that, I got drunk."

"Oh, I see. Drink to forget. I know a lot about that, been there myself."

I pull up outside Ellie's house. I turn to her, to tell her that she's home, but her head is resting against the window.

She's finally asleep, and I don't think I'll be able to wake her for a long time.

I turn the keys out of the ignition and sigh.

She's a hard one to handle.

"What are we going to do about you, Ellie Duke?"

9

ELLIE

I WAKE up to the smell of bacon and eggs. The warm scent fills my nostrils, making me drool before I even open my eyes.

And I also wake up to a raging headache of a hangover.

"Rich," I softly coo. Calling out to my ex-husband is an instinct I can't let go of. "You're making me breakfast?"

I blink, and that's when I realize I'm not in my own bed. I'm not in my apartment in Chicago, and I'm certainly not in my beach house.

Shit.

I jump out of the bed. I look down at myself. I'm still wearing the clothes I went out to town in last night, minus my shoes. I rush over to the nearest mirror to see myself in the reflection.

I look like a mess. My makeup is all runny and dried. My hair appears like it's been through a paddock.

I don't even remember how I got here, in this bedroom.

Where am I?

And then I catch another whiff of the cooking breakfast. *Downstairs.*

Carefully trying to not trip over myself, I slowly head down the stairs towards the source of the smell.

Yep, this is definitely not my beach house.

My suspicions are confirmed when I stagger into the kitchen and see my neighbor standing by the pan, cooking the bacon and eggs I'm drooling for.

And, as I've come to expect from him, he's topless.

"You?" I ask as I approach the kitchen counter.

Dec turns to me. He doesn't seem surprised to see me. He points to the stool next to his kitchen counter nonchalantly.

"Take a seat," he says. "Breakfast is almost ready."

"Breakfast?"

"I was half-expecting you to keep snoring all year, Sleeping Beauty."

I would refuse his command to sit, but I am *so* tired. I have no more resistance in me. I fall onto the stool and groan.

"What happened last night?" I ask, my memory hazy.

Dec's attention is on the food. "You were having a lot of fun singing your heart out in front of everyone in this small town."

Right. That.

"Oh, God."

"And then you decided to end your amazing act by falling down headfirst."

"Really? I don't remember that."

"I'm not surprised. It was pretty impressive. And it was pretty impressive you avoided splitting your head open."

"Great."

Dec snorts. "Do you usually get drunk and sing Journey?" he asks.

"I don't try to make a habit of it, no," I reply.

"I was going to leave you there on the ground, but then I thought maybe you do deserve some manners, even if you never properly thanked me for fixing your sink."

"Don't start this again. Please be gentle with me. I have the worst hangover in history."

"I don't doubt that."

"Then what happened?" I ask. "Did I vomit all over you or something?"

"Nothing as bad as that. I drove you back here. And now it's breakfast."

A horrible thought crosses my mind.

"We didn't, you know," I say. "We didn't have... *sex*, did we?"

I practically whisper the word like it's a curse.

Dec throws his head back and laughs.

"Look, I may be some weird dude who's nearly thirty and lives on his own in a shack by the beach, but I'm not horny enough to try anything with a girl that was as drunk as you were."

I suddenly feel something soft brush against my leg. Fur. I yelp and look down. It's Dec's dog. She stares up at me expectedly.

"Um. Hi," I say to the animal, my heart beating out of my chest in shock.

"Yeah, she really likes you," Dec comments. "Plus, she probably thinks you'll feed her some bacon."

"Yeah?"

"How about you do it?" Dec reaches into the pan, tears off a bit of bacon, and chucks it over to me.

I offer it out to Brandy. She gobbles it down eagerly, making me giggle.

"See? She likes you."

"Yeah, she isn't that much of a monster."

"Now you think so?"

"Sure," I reply.

"You're not too hungover for breakfast?"

"No, I'm starving."

"Here you go."

Dec serves out breakfast. It looks *amazing*, especially to my tired and strained eyes.

"You really don't have to do this for me," I say, staring at the full delicious plate in front of me.

"You're my guest, Ellie," Dec replies, pulling up another stool next to mine. "Stop blabbering and eat up."

And then I remember.

Last night in the car. What I said.

Shit.

I drop my knife and fork back onto the plate.

"Was I telling you... *things* last night?" I nervously ask my neighbor, cringing hard at my memories.

"Yeah, some things."

"What kind of things?"

"Oh, you know. Your divorce. Chicago. All that stuff. I could probably write your biography after all the truth bombs you were letting off in my passenger seat."

"Oh god."

Dec smiles and pats my hand. "Don't worry, it was nothing crazy. You were pretty funny. I like that."

His hand lingers on mine for just a moment too long. I feel the sparks between us. I look up into Dec's eyes and I see the flame of desire hidden in them.

I bet he can see the desire in mine.

It all lasts for the briefest of moments before he's pulling away from me, back to his plate and his eyes drop away.

I gotta say something to break the tension.

"Jesus. I'm sorry you had to hear all that."

"Well, I should be the one who's sorry. You seem to be

going through a pretty crazy time," Dec replies, taking a bite of bacon. "Do you remember telling me your favorite flowers?"

"No. Really? Oh, no."

"Yellow chrysanthemums, if my memory serves me right. It's all nothing to be ashamed of. You're a fun drunk, Ellie."

"Yeah, sure. Fun. I might as well shout out my life story from the rooftops."

"I know it isn't my place," Dec says quietly. "But you seemed very sad. I know you're going through a tough time at the moment."

I shrug. "I guess so."

"If you ever need someone to talk to, I'm here," he says.

I look up at him. His eyes are so sweet, so full of tenderness. He brought me safely home, and he's cooked me breakfast. He's different from the rough and dumb surfer boy I initially thought he was. "Um. Thanks, Dec."

We finish the rest of breakfast, me still cringing hard at what happened last night. I offer to wash up, but Dec refuses to let me near his sink.

"You sure?" I ask.

He stares at me deep in the eyes and I feel that sudden longing again. The longing for his warm, gentle touch on my hand.

I think he can feel it too.

"I'm sure, Ellie. You're my guest."

I gulp. I feel sweaty. I see the way he looks at me and I can't stand it.

I just want to reach out and touch his smooth, bare chest.

No, Ellie. Don't think about guys. Don't think about Dec that way.

I step back. "I hope you don't mind me snooping

around, then?" I ask.

I need an excuse to get away from him for a moment. To catch my breath before I do something rash. Something I might regret. Something like kissing his soft, inviting lips.

"Go right ahead," he replies, turning back to the sink.

Surely, he feels the tension too? He's just so cool about it, though.

As he wipes down the plates, I wander around his house. He's a clean guy. Very simple living. He doesn't even have a TV.

I stroll over to the bookshelf. Lots of cool photo albums of world-class surfers adorn his shelves.

On the top shelf is a picture frame. I bring it down to have a look. It's a photo of Dec and a blonde-haired woman, holding each other with the sun behind them. They're both smiling. It feels very authentic, as if they didn't even know someone was taking a photo of them.

"Who's this?" I ask Dec from across the room, raising up the picture frame.

It takes him a moment to register what I mean, and then he averts his gaze.

"That's my wife," he says softly.

"Oh. What's her name?"

"I don't really want to talk about her."

His directness throws me off.

"Why not?"

"I just don't."

"Well, I'd like to meet her. If you'll let us."

Dec doesn't say anything. He turns around, showing me his back.

Rude.

Have I touched a nerve?

I see he doesn't want to talk about anything else, so I put the frame back where I found it.

"Well, thanks for breakfast," I say. "And thanks for getting me back okay last night."

He looks back at me and just nods. No other reply.

Right, so showing him a picture of his wife makes him moody?

He continues not saying anything, so I awkwardly leave. I shut the door and stand outside his place for a moment, expecting him to call out or say something, but he doesn't.

Alright then. Be all moody. Be all weird just because I want to talk about the wife you're hiding away.

I walk across the beach back to my place.

My hands shake. There was so much unexpected sexual tension between the surfer and me just then. Him, topless, making me breakfast like that – taking care of me like that in such a tender way – stirred something deep within me.

I lick my lips.

What would it be like to kiss him, I wonder? Would he taste of the ocean?

No, Ellie. Stop this.

I can't be climbing straight into the bed of a man I just met. I'm a new divorcee. I came out here to escape men and heartbreak. I'm not going through that again so soon.

But I know no matter how much I say *no*, a hidden part of me desperately wants to know the feel of Dec Page's exposed chest.

And I think he wants me too.

But then there was the picture of his wife. His hidden wife. What was that about?

Who is she, and why hasn't he spoken about her before?

Why haven't I met her yet?

Does she even live here? Are they divorced?

And why does my head spin when I think of him?

So many questions, and I don't think I'll be getting answers anytime soon.

10

ELLIE

I turn on my shower, praying that the thing doesn't explode on me. Surprisingly, it doesn't. Instead of an explosion, water spurts out the nozzle. Warm water.

It works!

I step into the shower stall and begin to wash.

I've just returned from Dec's and I really need a shower. I still feel crappy from the night before. My head is still raging with the hangover. All I need right now is a good clean and a soft bed.

I groan and close my eyes, lifting my head back to take the full force of the water. It's refreshing.

And then I hear some kind of clanging. It's coming from inside the wall behind the shower. It's like something's banging behind there.

I open my eyes and turn off the shower. Steam clogs up the bathroom.

I poke my head out of the shower stall and quietly listen.

It's still there.

A low banging. But it's coming from downstairs now.

I quickly wrap the towel around me and dart downstairs, worried.

This is a crazy old beach house. It could be anything.

I rush into the kitchen.

The banging was coming from my sink.

My sink that is now overflowing. Again. Water pools on the floor around my feet. It's freaking scary.

"Shit, shit, shit."

There's only one thing I can do.

I run into the living room where I left my phone. I frantically scroll through my contacts until the handyman's number that Jen gave me yesterday flashes up.

I quickly send off a message.

Hi! So, this is super random, but any chance of coming around now? My sink is overfilling, and I am in urgent need of assistance.

I know he was supposed to come by this afternoon to quote his services, but I really do need him now. There's no chance in hell I can fix this sink.

This whole building could collapse or something.

It's either pester the handyman or go opposite and ask Dec for help, and I ain't doing that.

Nope. Not him.

My phone pings. It's the handyman.

Coming around now.

* * *

THERE'S a knock on the door only a few minutes later.

Wow, he's fast.

I haven't even got out of my towel yet. I'm naked except for it. I'm just standing here in the living room, basically

65

exposed except for a bit of fabric loosely wrapped around my body.

I turn from the knock on the door back to look inside the kitchen. I bite my lip. The sink is really overflowing now with no end in sight. I don't have time to get him to wait whilst I get changed.

Damn.

I'm just going to have to answer the door with my just my towel wrapped around me.

Great. Just great.

I open up to him.

But it isn't a handyman that's standing there on my porch.

It's Dec.

I nearly shriek out in surprise. I grip the towel, pulling it around me even tighter.

And just like this morning, he's still not wearing a shirt.

"What are you doing here?" I ask. "I'm practically naked."

Dec chuckles. I've realized he likes to laugh at me.

"Don't worry," he says. "I'm here for the sink, not to see you naked."

The sink? How does he know?

Oh.

"You're the handyman," I exclaim, finally getting it. "Blue Haven's handyman."

A big smile spreads across my neighbor's face.

"I thought you knew," he says.

"No?"

"Well, I am."

I nearly fall to the ground in shock. "Oh, god."

"You can stand there all day, or you can let me in, Ellie. I'd like to be able to do my job."

"Oh. Right."

I move to the side and Dec steps in, carrying a toolbox. He makes his way into the kitchen and starts to work on the sink.

He crouches down and gets in deep amongst the pipes, giving me a clear view of his perfectly shaped ass, just like yesterday when I first arrived.

And just like yesterday, I find it impossible not to admire his body.

God, he's gorgeous.

I watch him as he works, as he screws and hammers, until the sink is overflowing no more. No more bubbling water. No more leakage. It's like he's worked a miracle.

A handsome handyman knight come to save the damsel in distress.

He sighs and pulls himself out from under the sink. He looks up at me.

"Okay, that should hold it for now."

"Thank you, Dec."

There's a long pause between us, just like there was this morning. He looks at me and I look at him. I bite my lip.

Damn. This tension. It's making me dizzy.

I wonder what he's like under those shorts. I mean, I've seen the rest of him. If his tight muscles and perfect abs are anything to go by, then the evidence is pretty clear that there must be something *big* going on under there.

Something I might like to get my lips around of.

"So, you were messaging me?" he eventually asks, and I quickly snap out of my illicit daydreams.

"Um. Yeah. Before I knew you were, well... *you.*"

"I'm still me," he says.

Yeah, he's really enjoying this, isn't he?

"I can't believe you're the handyman Jen told me about. I should've put two and two together."

"So, you want to hire me to help renovate this place?" he asks.

I take in a deep breath. I did think the handyman would be a different person to the man that lives a hundred yards from me. Would having him work here be a problem?

I don't know.

But who else can I turn to? Jen said he was the best in town. It seems like it's either Dec or pack up and go back to Chicago.

"Please," I reply. "If it isn't going to be a problem."

"Great, but this place is going to need a lot of work." He glances up at the dodgy-looking ceiling. "A *lot* of work."

"You're telling me."

"But I'll be happy to do it. For a fee, of course."

"Of course."

"But," he winks. "I can do it for mate's rates. *Neighbor's* rates."

"Okay, thanks." I look down at the towel wrapped around my body. "And maybe next time I won't be so naked."

Dec laughs again. "Yeah, that might help."

So. My neighbor is going to be my handyman?

My sexy, *irresistible* neighbor. The one that I promised myself I wouldn't lust after? He's the one I'm going to have to watch, topless, as he fixes up this beach house with his thick biceps and perfect jawline? Yeah. Him.

The same guy who told me he has a wife this morning.

The wife I haven't met.

Boy, Ellie, you've really got yourself in a quagmire here.

11

ELLIE

THE SAND IS soft under my feet as I jog across the beach. The soft texture makes it hard to run. I have to really work hard to push on.

I face the ocean. The blue water shines in the afternoon sun. It's been a few hours since Dec came over to fix my sink.

I still can't get over this place I've moved to. It's hot, and it's always sunny, full of green nature and the beach. A little slice of paradise. Such a difference to rainy old Chicago.

I look out over the water. It's so inviting. The waves foam and crash on the shore.

I'm going to go for a little swim once I make it back home.

I'm enjoying taking long runs on the beach. It feels better than being stuck on some treadmill in a windowless downtown gym back home. This place is good for me. I'm starting to come around to the idea that it was right for me to go on vacation.

I breathe in the fresh air and power on through the soft sand, feeling the effort shape me. I need to get back into my old body. A week of feasting on junk food since Rich divorced me has left me feeling like a lump of dough. It's like I'm trying to exercise out the memories of my ex-husband.

There's a vibration in my pocket. It's my phone.

I unzip my specialty spandex running pants and take it out.

MOM.

I come to a stop by the shoreline and answer her call.

"Hi, Mom."

"Ellie! How are you? How's New Haven?"

"It's *Blue* Haven, and yeah, I'm actually alright. Well, everything's alright apart from the beach house."

"The beach house? What's wrong with it?"

There's panic in her voice.

I laugh. "Everything. Where to start? It's all crumbling apart, Mom."

"Really?"

"I think I'm going to really need to roll my sleeves up for this. It's going to be a big job."

"Well, that's never stopped you before, Ellie, has it?"

"No. Never."

"You've always liked a big task," Mom says.

"Tell me about it."

"Are you going to get help?"

I turn to look at Dec's house.

"Um. Yeah. I think so."

"And how's the town?" she asks.

I laugh again. "Small."

"Of course it is. What did you expect?"

"I honestly don't know, but it's actually perfect for me. It's practically deserted around here, Mom. I feel

70

like I can breathe free away from all the people in the city."

"Good, good," she replies. "And the big question I have to ask you is, have you met any men?"

"*Mom*. Really? You're asking that now?"

"Why not?"

"Mom, the love of my life asked for a divorce, like, literally a week ago," I reply, frowning. "The very last thing I'm thinking of is men."

"Well, there's no time to waste to get back into the dating pool."

"*Mom*."

I can hear the glee in her voice as she pokes at me from the other side of the country. She loves teasing me.

"Ellie, I am sure there's some hunk just waiting to be snatched up in New Haven, and you're the woman to do it."

"There are honestly no men in *Blue* Haven, Mom," I reply. "Zero. And besides, I'm here to redo this property and nothing else. I am not planning on doing something silly like falling in love."

"Oh, you have *everything* planned for in your tight little life, don't you, sweetie?"

"Yes. You know me."

"No time for anything spontaneous."

"No."

"No time for anything fun."

I roll my eyes. "You know me."

"Well, sometimes you can't factor in love. It doesn't work for our schedules."

"Yes, Mom."

"Even yours, Ellie. How about you find someone?"

"No, Mom."

"What if Rich wants you back?"

I pause. "What do you mean?"

"What if he apologizes and says he made a mistake?"

"Mom," I reply. "He's never going to do that."

"Would you go back to him if he does, though?"

I sigh. "No."

"You sure?"

"I'm sure, Mom."

That's enough of that now.

I know she's just trying to be helpful in the way Mom likes to be, but it's messing with my head. I don't want to think about Rich, and I certainly don't want to think about getting back together with him.

Maybe I don't want to think about him because I know that maybe I would go back to him if he asked me to, that maybe I might crawl back to his sorry ass if he grovels on his hands and knees enough.

And that's a scary thought.

"Right, well, I've got to go back to it," I say. I want to end this conversation quickly. "Walls don't get painted by themselves, you know."

"Find yourself a man, Ellie."

"No, Mom."

"Come on."

"I'm hanging up now, okay? No more man talk."

I hang up and bend over, panting. I'm more exhausted from the run than I thought.

I really do need to get back into shape.

I sigh. Mom is really on a roll about men at the moment. Oh, she really does love a bit of drama. Serves me right for opening up to her over the last week.

But I ain't telling her shit.

I look out over the waves. There's a black speck on the horizon, bobbling in and out of view.

Dec.

I squint to see him clearer. He's surfing. He dances on the waves. A natural in the water.

He's probably topless out there as well. Does that man even own a shirt?

Look, I lied to Mom when I said there were no men.

There *is* a man in Blue Haven. A man who attracts my eye, no matter how much I try to avoid him.

And I bet if she knew about him, Mom would absolutely love Dec Page.

But the man is married. I saw the photo of his wife at his house this morning. He explicitly *told* me she was his wife. Therefore, he's not mine to pursue. He has a wife, which means he is off-market. I'm not a home-wrecker, and I don't plan to be.

So that settles it. I was right on the call with Mom.

No men for me in Blue Haven.

12

ELLIE

I'M MAKING a fruit smoothie for myself when I see Dec through my kitchen window, crossing the beach towards me. I am making an absolute mess of the drink. I finish slicing the banana and tip it into the blender before I rush to the door, opening it as Dec raises his hand to knock.

"Oh, hello," he says, startled, when I appear in front of him. He blinks at me. It is very satisfying to snap him out of his chilled surfer vibe for once. It feels like payback for him, always getting me flustered by never wearing shirts.

And, once again, he isn't wearing one now. Typical.

I lean on the doorframe and try to ignore his sexy, dripping wet body. It's very hard not to stare. "Hello, Dec. Been surfing?"

"Yeah. Good waves today."

"I saw," I reply, smiling at how shocked he still is from me suddenly opening the door. "You like your surfing, don't you?"

"Always have. How are you settling in?"

"Well, there's been no more leakages so far, and I'm trying to make a smoothie. Pretty unsuccessfully so far."

Dec pokes his head around the door, taking a look at my messy blender.

"You don't need my help at all," he says sarcastically with a smile.

"What can I do for you, Dec?"

He offers out a piece of paper.

"What's this?" I ask.

"Have a look," he replies.

I take it from him. It's a list he's handwritten.

"These are the things I'm going to need to start work on the house."

"You've already written them down?" I ask.

"I'm fast."

"Okay, so where can I get these things from?"

"Morgana Hardware in town," he replies. "The owner Jen there is amazing. She'll be able to help you."

"Yeah, she is amazing."

"You've met her already?" Dec asks, raising an eyebrow.

"She's the one who gave me your number."

He nods and scoffs at the thought. "I see. How very sneaky of her."

"You know her?"

"Yeah, I know her pretty well."

"How?"

Dec shakes his head. "We go way back."

Hm. He's being mysterious about her. Maybe I can coax some more info from Jen.

"I think I'll get these things today."

"Great, then we can get started on this house sooner."

And then I remember.

"Actually, I'll have to walk into town, thanks to me

leaving my car there last night," I say. "You want to tag along?"

Maybe I can ask him some questions this time after I babbled out my entire life story last night. Get to know him. Find out about this mysterious wife of his.

Dec shakes his head slowly. "Sorry, but no."

"Why not?"

There's a long pause. Dec turns to look at the waves in the distance.

He eventually speaks after a few moments, his voice barely above a whisper. "I'm off to see my wife."

"Yeah?"

"Today's our anniversary."

"Nice. Congratulations."

This goddamn mysterious wife again. Who is the heck is she?

"Thanks," he replies, stepping away from the door. "Let me know when you get the stuff. You've got my number."

"I will."

He turns and goes, heading back to his place. It's so fast. He clearly doesn't want to hang around.

He clearly doesn't want me to ask about his wife.

It's strange I haven't even met her yet.

Weird.

Where does she even live? It'll be unusual, but not crazy that she would live in some other place. I guess I shouldn't judge. Different people have different relationships.

I close the door and head back into the kitchen. I turn on the blender and watch Dec through the window slip into his house.

I want to find out more about this guy.

* * *

"So," I say to the store owner. "Dec's made me a list."

"Has he?" Jen asks.

I hand over the piece of paper over to Jen and she scans it, her brows furrowed.

"He said to give it to you," I comment, tapping the counter absentmindedly.

She raises an eyebrow at the mention of his name, just like Dec had done earlier with hers. "Did he now?"

"He said that you're the person to go to."

"I think we should have everything here," she says, biting her lip and casting a quick look around the shop. "We might have to do a little searching around for some stuff, though. It might take a while."

"I'm happy to wait."

It took me longer than I thought to walk into town, but it was relieving to find my car where I parked it yesterday. I shivered when I saw it. The car sitting there was a stark reminder of how stupidly drunk I got last night.

And how those series of events led me to waking up in Dec's bed this morning.

Jen turns towards the back of the shop. "Aaron?"

The little boy appears, smiling at me. I smile back.

Jen hands him the piece of paper. "I want you to collect everything listed on here and bag them up in the back. Any problems and you let me know, understood?"

"Yep."

"Good boy."

"Thanks, Aaron," I say as he sprints around the corner.

"This should take an hour," Jen says. "I think. It shouldn't take no more than two if you want a little walk around town and come back then."

I nod.

And then I have an idea.

"Are you busy right now, Jen?"

"Well, not really."

"Do you have to be here?" I ask.

"I don't have to be. Why?"

"Maybe you can join me for a bit. We could go for a walk."

"Right."

"You see, I don't really know anyone in town, and it'll be nice to talk to someone," I say. "And, hey, I can buy you a coffee."

Jen shrugs. "Say no more. You had me at coffee." She turns towards the back again. "You okay if I leave for a bit, Aaron?"

"Yep," a tiny voice calls out.

"You'll be okay on your own? You have my phone number."

"I will be fine," comes the defiant voice from the back. "Jeez."

Jen smiles at me. "I guess the boss is allowing me a short break. Let's go before he changes his mind."

13

ELLIE

"How LONG HAVE you lived in Blue Haven, Jen?" I ask as we exit the cafe, takeaway coffees in hand. The two of us stroll down the main street of the town, the sun shining brightly in the sky above us.

"My whole life," she replies. "My sister and I were born and raised here."

The town is busy today. Well, as busy as it can be, considering its size. A few cars drive up the main street. There are a few shoppers. One or two people I recognize from the bar last night.

I hope they don't recognize me.

"You've never thought about leaving?" I ask Jen, taking a sip of coffee.

"Why would I leave? I love it here, and all my memories are here," she replies, looking around. "Although Blue Haven can feel like a tiny world sometimes."

"I bet it does."

"Yeah. You're from Chicago, right?" she asks me.

"Yep."

"Big city there."

"It's been a bit of a culture shock moving from there to Blue Haven," I reply. "So, you would say it's a pretty tight community here, then?"

Jen laughs, the first time I've seen her do so. "Tight is too weak a term for it. *Suffocating* is better. People love to talk and spread rumors around here, especially behind your back. I'm not a big fan of that kind of behavior."

"It's not that bad, is it?"

She laughs again. I like the way she laughs; her features all light up. "No, I'm only joking. Although I have already heard of your little stint as a pop star in the bar last night."

I'm flabbergasted. I can barely keep my coffee down and not snort it out of my nose. "What? How have you heard about that? It was only last night, and I didn't know anyone knew who I was."

She shrugs. "As I said, people around here really like to talk, and they can spot an out-of-towner from miles off. You're big news already. You're the girl who's come to fix the old beach house."

"Great, so everyone already knows about me?"

"Don't worry, it isn't too bad," Jen replies. "Blue Haven isn't too bad. It just depends on the people, and there are some good people here. You've just got to find them. And stay away from the gossipers."

"And Declan Page?" I ask. "Is he one of the good people?"

A faint smile crosses Jen's lips. "Ah, Dec. He's a different type. Your neighbor has one hell of a story."

I reach for her arm, excited that I might be divulged some gossip about this man. "What is it? What's his deal?"

Jen shakes her head. "I don't feel like it's right talking

about him when he isn't here. I don't want to be one of those rumor-spreaders."

"No, Jen. You *must* tell me now. You can't tease me like that and not say anything."

She winks at me. "You'd fit in quite nicely here in Blue Haven, Ellie Duke. Forcing me to gossip like this."

I giggle. "Tell me. Please. I better know my neighbor after all when he's living so close. He might be a serial killer for all I know. A girl's gotta keep safe."

"Okay. Fine." Jen brushes her hair back like she's physically getting ready to hit me with some truth-bombs. "He's married, you know."

"Yeah, he told me."

"Well, he's actually a widower."

I stop.

Oh shit.

All of it makes sense now. The fact his wife doesn't live with him, the fact he's uneasy talking about her. It's because she's passed away, that's why.

God. I've been so insensitive.

Jen stares at my astonished expression.

"I didn't know that. And he spoke to me about her. I feel like an idiot."

"I thought so. I can imagine it's awkward trying to tell someone you're a widower."

"God, I really am such a massive idiot. I've been bumbling around his house talking about her, and thinking about her, and all this time she's passed away? And he didn't even tell me?"

"Don't worry, I know Dec, and I'm sure he doesn't care."

I tut at myself for all the thoughts I've had about him this last day.

Have I been lusting after a widower on the day of his anniversary?

"So, what happened with his wife?"

I feel bad for asking this, but curiosity is killing me. Jen doesn't seem to mind. She takes a long sip of her coffee and nods.

"A car crash. It was pretty shocking. Absolutely not her fault at all. It happened three years ago outside of town on the highway. Dec wasn't there, and I don't think he's ever forgiven himself for it. I think he's still getting over it now."

"Something like that would take a lifetime to heal," I reply softly. "He told me it's his anniversary today."

"Yeah, I guess it would be. Sad day."

"I am such an idiot for asking him about her."

"You wouldn't believe in the number of women who've tried to date him since the accident. The whole female percentage of town has, and so has one or two of the men. All have failed miserably. He's Blue Haven's hottest property."

"I can see why."

Jen raises an eyebrow. "Oh, is there something going on between you two?" she asks conspiratorially.

I laugh and shake my head. "Oh, no. Not at all. Nothing other than me being super weird about his wife. He seems happy enough on his own. Just him and his dog."

"Yep. Ever since the accident."

"How did he and his wife meet?"

"They were high school sweethearts. Love at first sight and all of that."

"Right."

"He scattered her ashes on a cliff overlooking a beach not far from here. He still goes there to talk to her."

"I guess people deal with stuff in their own way."

"Yeah. I could never go to that cliff. Instead, I

remember her with this." Jen says, pulling her shirt down far enough that I can see a name tattooed below her collarbone.

KENDRA.

"I'm her sister," Jen says. "*Was* her sister."

For the second time in a few minutes, I stop.

Shit. Again.

"Oh, I'm sorry, Jen. I didn't know that."

"It's okay. There's no need to apologize for anything. Kendra is hard to talk about, for me and for Dec."

"Wow. I can imagine."

"We've both learned to process our grief in different ways," she continues. "Dec keeps everything to himself, and me? Well... I've got my shop. I'm happy enough. Although a day doesn't go by when I don't think of her. That's probably why I'll never leave Blue Haven. There are just too many memories of her here."

"Of course."

Jen wipes a solitary tear away from her eye. "Sorry to get a bit weird and emotional."

I wrap an arm around her. "No, don't be sorry."

"I guess today is a weird day, it being Dec and Kendra's anniversary and all."

"I guess so," I reply, rubbing her back. "So that makes Dec your..."

"Brother-in-law. Yes."

"And you're still close?" I ask.

"Yeah, we're still close."

"Is that why you gave me his number for the renovation work?"

Jen smiles. "Yeah, a little bit of nepotism was at play, but I was right in saying he's the best in town."

"Sure, sure," I laugh.

We pass by Blue Haven's market. A few stalls with

various random items for sale. We browse through them, not finding anything worth buying.

It's nice to meet someone like Jen. She's authentic. Straight-talking. I like her. If she lived in Chicago, I can imagine we'd be close friends.

We get to the last stall in the tiny market, and my eyes are automatically drawn to a Polaroid camera hanging on a stand.

"I've always wanted one of those," I say to Jen. "Something not digital to take some memories with."

"Why don't you get it?" she suggests.

Spontaneous purchases are not my thing. I'm so careful with money. Every time I buy something, I run a checklist of pros and cons in my head. It usually takes a lot for me to commit money to something.

But fuck it.

I'm here in Blue Haven. My lifestyle has changed.

"You know what? I will," I say to Jen. "Just because I'm here and I guess I should be taking more photos."

"Do it."

I hand over the cash to the seller, and the camera is in my hands.

Maybe I need a bit of spontaneity in my life.

* * *

I sit down on my porch and watch the sunset, wine glass in hand. The sky is a fiery blood orange tonight. The ocean is dark. All I can hear are the comforting repetitive sounds of the waves crashing on the shore.

It's so relaxing.

Today has been a good day.

I paid Jen and Aaron for the goods, drove them back

home, and cooked a hearty dinner for myself. A whole lot of pasta.

And now I'm sitting on this porch enjoying the view.

A deserted beach. No one else around. People would pay a lot of dough to be sitting here right now, and I have this view for free.

I sigh happily and take a sip of white wine.

I spot two shapes farther down the beach. Dec walking his dog.

I sit still for a moment and watch him stroll across the sand.

I think about what Jen told me in town today. About his wife. The pain he must have gone through, what he must *still* be going through.

How do you even get over something like that? I probably wouldn't. I can't even get over a stupid divorce.

I watch Dec as he walks with his confident strides. He's a quiet man. A man who doesn't need much. It's admirable, in a way.

He doesn't need much, but he's lost his woman. That must be the hardest thing of all.

And I thought I had problems.

14

DEC

I WAKE up in the middle of the night to some furious knocking downstairs. The sound fills my ears.

Someone knocking on my front door.

I leap out of bed in a panic, breathing shallowly. I'm in a panic.

No, hang on. There's no noise.

I stop.

Maybe I was dreaming it. I've gotten out of bed for nothing.

Knock knock knock.

No, someone really is down there.

But who'll be knocking on *my* door at this time? I live in the middle of nowhere.

I hear Brandy start to bark downstairs. By now she'll be at the front door, ready to attack any intruder.

I reach under my bed for the baseball bat I keep for situations like these. I grip it tightly in my hand as I race down the stairs. My dog is indeed crouched, ready to pounce, in the hallway.

"Who is it?" I cry out to the locked door.

"It's me."

Wait, I know who that is.

I hush Brandy. She whimpers but sits still.

I unlock the door.

And just as I expect, Ellie Duke is standing there on my porch. Her hair is wet. Glistening. Sweat, I guess.

"Hey," I say to her, my heart pounding. I take in a deep breath to calm myself.

It's just Ellie, I tell myself. I need to cool down. I was just ready to bash in someone's brains with the bat a moment ago.

"Hi," she replies.

"What's wrong?" I ask.

She shrugs and smiles, bashful, at me. "You were right. It is too hot to sleep at night."

I sigh and shake my head. "This is what you've woken me up for? This is what's made you come across the beach in the middle of the night to pound at my door for?"

"Um. Yep."

"You didn't get a fan, I guess? Just like I told you to?"

Ellie bites her lip guiltily. The movement makes me want to grab her hair and pull her face towards me in a kiss. I want to bite that lower lip until she's biting it no more.

"Nope," she says.

"And I thought you were smart."

"Give a city girl a break."

I sigh. My heartbeat slows. I am not upset she's here. I guess she's here for one reason. "You want to stay over for tonight? I have air-con."

"Oh, yes, please."

I laugh and step aside. "Come on in then, city girl."

Ellie skips into my house, her cheeks red with shame.

Yeah, she deserves to feel remorse for not listening to my advice.

I follow her into the living room.

"Tomorrow I'm getting you a fan," I say.

She frowns. "There's no need for that."

"I don't want you to burn up over there," I reply. I point at the sweat dripping down her neck.

"Ha. Yes, I was starting to burn. I was worried I might actually be melting or something. I can't believe a night can get so hot."

"I guess you don't reach these kinds of temperatures up where you're from."

"Nope."

"Do you want some water?" I ask. "You must be so hot."

"Yes, please."

I go into the kitchen and pour her a glass at the sink. I take it back into the living room and hand it to her.

Our fingers touch as she takes the glass from me. A shiver runs down my body as I feel her soft, warm hands on mine.

And then we part. We only touched for the briefest of moments, but it still feels like heaven. I haven't been touched for a long time.

She downs the water in one go. I'm impressed. She must've been really sweating before she decided to knock on my door.

"Thirsty?"

"Yep. It was getting so hot," she pants.

"Help yourself to a clean towel in the bathroom if you'd like. Give yourself a splash of water."

"Thanks."

She disappears into the bathroom and I ready the couch

for me to sleep on. I get a spare pillow from my room and dump a sheet over the couch.

"What are you doing?" Ellie asks me. She's stepped in behind me from the bathroom.

"You can have my bed and I'll sleep down here."

"Nonsense. Follow me," she replies. She turns and walks upstairs, not waiting for me. I quickly follow her up into my bedroom. She stands by my bed, looking at it. "There's more than enough space for two here."

She points at it.

I can't disagree. She's right. My bed is pretty big, and it can technically fit us both in it.

"You sure?" I ask her.

"As long as you stay on your side and I stay on mine, I think we'll be alright."

"Only if you're okay."

"I doubt you're going to roll over and squash me in your sleep," she laughs, punching me playfully on my exposed pec. Her touch reignites something in me. A hunger.

I swallow and try to suppress that feeling.

Not now. Not here. Not with her.

I clear my throat and quickly change the subject. "Did you get the stuff from town?" I ask.

"Yep, and I spoke to Jen."

I raise an eyebrow. "Yeah? What did she say?"

"Oh, she told me all about you."

"What did she tell you about me?" I ask, flustered.

"It was nothing."

I don't believe her.

"Jen likes to talk. A lot. She's sly like that," I say. "I bet she really let loose."

"My lips are sealed," Ellie replies.

"Great. Now you're gonna have me guessing what she said to you all night."

Ellie laughs and pulls down the bed covers, patting the mattress. "Come on, get into bed."

Eyeing her suspiciously, I slide in next to her. My bed definitely has room for both of us.

We lie in stillness for a moment. All I can hear is her breathing next to me.

Ellie turns to me and sighs.

"Thanks for this, Dec. It's much cooler in here."

"It's no problem, Ellie."

"Goodnight."

"Night."

I switch off the bedside lamp, plunging us into darkness.

I guess I'm going to have to spend a restless night next to the woman I've been thinking so much about. How will I cope?

I lie there for a long time, listening to my breathing as my chest rises and falls. I can feel Ellie's hot breath gently blow against my bare shoulder.

I think of her. So close to me, but unable to be seen in the dark. This strange city girl who's flown into my beach like a whirlwind and who might have stolen my heart.

We're so different. The surfer dude and the uptight chick. And yet I feel a connection to her. A connection I haven't with someone felt for a long, long time.

I don't even know what my type is, but Ellie, with her athletic body and wavy brown hair, has completely dominated my thoughts ever since I saw her attempting to sing *Don't Stop Believing* back in that bar.

And now she's in my bed, and I can't even see her in the darkness.

But I do feel her. I feel her arm moving across the bedsheets as she wraps it around my torso. I feel her body shuffle up beside me until she's cuddling me.

Wow.

Being so close, she must be able to feel my heartbeat. If she did, she'll feel it pounding.

I lie still with her body wrapped around mine as she slowly drifts off to sleep.

I've not had a woman in my bed for a long time. After my wife's accident, I don't think I ever could.

But this actually feels right. Ellie feels right.

Especially when she's wrapped around me like this.

I don't dare to move. I don't want her to slide away from me. I want to stay like this forever.

It takes me a long time to fall asleep, but when I do, it's a deep one, full of dreams about this girl lying next to me.

15

DEC

I WAKE up looking at Ellie. Our faces are so close they are nearly touching. I let out a long sigh as I scan my eyes over her beautiful face. She looks so peaceful when she's sleeping. Like a cute kitten. Her skin seems so soft, and her body is so warm. She's so close and so inviting and so cuddly that I just want to reach out and stroke her cheeks.

I can't believe she's in my bed. Even now, last night feels like a dream. A wonderful dream. Her knocking on my door in the middle of the night. Her needing me. How I took care of her, and then how she commanded me to sleep next to her in the same bed. It felt so good with her pushing up against me and wrapping her arms around my body all night as we slept.

And now I don't ever want her to leave this bed.

As I look at her, Ellie's eyes flutter open. It's as if she's waking up at exactly the same time as me. As if us being in such close proximity puts our bodies into sync.

She stares at me and I stare back. We don't talk.

Instead, we just lose ourselves in each other's gaze.

The morning light streams through the cracks in my curtains, illuminating the room in a soft golden haze.

I smile and eventually speak. It's no louder than a soft whisper.

"Morning."

She takes in an extended breath.

"Morning," she replies in the same tone.

I slowly move even closer to her, sliding across the pillow until I'm a mere inch away from her face. I just simply have to do it, especially when she looks as pretty as she does now.

Ellie doesn't resist. She doesn't back away. She lets me get this close.

I notice her breathing speeds up, and so does mine, but she still doesn't move. She just continues staring at me with those lovely, big brown eyes of hers.

I lean in even closer.

We're so close now.

We're about to touch.

And then we're kissing.

It's explosive. Like it's a big bang. Like we've been gearing up for this for a long time.

She tastes sweet, and her lips are soft and welcoming.

We push up against each other. Her body snuggles into mine. I envelop her. My hand slides under the bedsheets. My finger delicately traces its tip down her back. I feel her shiver.

I close my eyes and submit myself to her touch. My cock is hard.

But then she's pulling away.

She breaks off from the kiss and quickly shuffles out of bed. She's out from under the bedsheets before I can even react.

"I can't," she whispers. "I can't."

I pull myself out of bed on the other side, giving her space.

"I'm sorry, Ellie, I just..."

"I know. I let you do that. It felt right."

"Yeah. Did you like it?" I ask gently.

She glances down at the ground. "It was amazing," she says softly.

"I thought so too."

But I realize my optimism is misplaced when Ellie shakes her head defiantly. "But it is wrong, Dec. So wrong to do what we just did. We're *neighbors*."

"Okay. We're neighbors, so what? It was just a kiss."

"Nothing is ever *just a kiss*, Dec. If left... unchecked, this could be an issue."

"It doesn't have to be an issue."

"Dec. Please. Don't make this any harder."

"I'm not trying to."

I don't have any words.

"I didn't mean it to be like this," she says, spluttering over her words. "When I came over, I didn't mean for this to happen. Last night, I..."

"It's okay, I know," I reply. She's confused, I get it. I can't make her understand.

"I was married just a few days ago. This all feels so fast."

I sit down on the bed. "I understand," I say, looking down at my hands.

We have moved fast. I moved too fast in kissing her, but yet it did feel *right* at the moment. It felt like something I had to do.

Otherwise, I knew I would regret it forever.

"It was silly," Ellie says.

"Yeah, silly."

She nods slowly. "I'm glad we both have the same view."

"Right."

"It was just something that happened in the heat of the moment. I hope we can still be friends," she says.

And there we go. *Friends*. The most painful word for me to possibly hear comes from Ellie's beautiful lips.

The one word I don't ever want to hear her say.

But now she's broken that seal, and I worry there's no going back.

"Yep," I reply softly. "Friends."

"I hope this doesn't change anything between us."

I smile. "It was just a kiss. It doesn't mean anything," I lie.

"Okay. You'll still help me with the house?"

"Don't worry, I'm going to help you with the house. In a professional capacity, of course. I'm not here to ruin a few months of good paid work over a moment of weakness one morning."

I try to keep it light, but my heart is shattered. This is the most pain I have felt for a very long time.

"Exactly."

"Good. Should we start today?" I ask.

Ellie shrugs. "I see why not."

"Perfect."

There's a long, awkward pause. I don't know what else there is to say. The air is stilted between us.

"I better be off," Ellie says, breaking the awkwardness. "I'll see you after breakfast?"

"I'll come over in an hour."

"Great."

She quickly scurries out of the room and heads out the front door.

And I feel like a total idiot. I've screwed up this lucrative fix-up job before it's even begun.

She's gone.

But she was never mine to begin with.

What the hell just happened?

I sigh and fall back on the bed. The mattress bounces under my weight. The room feels so empty without her. It's like all the air's been sucked out.

And now I'm alone. Again.

You're such a fool, Dec.

Yes, I am.

I was too bold. Too fast. And now I've potentially fucked this whole arrangement up.

I need to nip this all in the bud. I need to break the awkward tension between Ellie and me.

But I can't just simply turn up in an hour and start work on the house, not when there's this weird feeling between us.

Ugh.

What can I possibly do to repair this?

I lie still on the bed and think. I close my eyes, but even that doesn't erase the image of Ellie's lips from my mind. I can't get her out of my head.

What is wrong with you, Dec? Has she really burrowed in deep after only a few days?

I'm the loner. The weird surfer guy living on the edge of town with just his dog for company.

But then Ellie rode in, and now everything's changed.

Fuck.

I start to drift off to sleep. Unconsciousness is better than having to deal with this strange new pain.

But then I sit back up.

I have an idea.

I know what I can do to fix this.

16

ELLIE

I SHUT the door with a bang once I get inside my house from Dec's place. I fall back heavily on the doorframe and close my eyes.

Only one thought dominates my mind.

He kissed me. He kissed me. He kissed me.

And I kissed him back.

And even though I freaked out in that bedroom, even though I told him it was all wrong, that kiss still felt so goddamn right. His lips fitted perfectly around mine. I felt his hard cock brush against me, and my own body lusted so deeply for him. I could've easily slipped into asking him to fuck me right there and then.

And then where would I be?

What are you doing, Ellie? What have you got yourself into?

What had I explicitly told Mom on the phone just yesterday?

No men.

None.

And I had meant it when I told Mom that there were no men for me in Blue Haven. I am not here for that. It's the very last thing I need right now. Hell, I was still married to the love of my life just a few days ago.

I came here to fix up this beach house. Nothing more. I am not letting my heart get exposed and then broken by another man.

But. Still.

Declan.

I can't deny I felt something wonderful when he kissed me. My heart flew when our lips brushed. My body shivered with anticipation at his touch. I wondered what his cock would taste like.

Nope. Remember what you promised yourself, Ellie. No men.

I bang the back of my head against the door in frustration.

What a night that was.

What. A. Morning.

"You're crazy, Ellie. Certifiably insane."

I tut at myself and head into the kitchen to make breakfast. Anything to take my mind off over what just happened. I play loud music on my phone in a desperate attempt to fill my head with a sound other than Dec's soft breathing. I furiously wash my hands in the sink like I'm trying to wash away his delicate touch. I intensely focus on the fry-up instead of my mind's images of his naked chest mere inches from my own.

I sit down at my kitchen table and eat the food, trying to keep my mind blank.

But it takes a lot to erase the lingering memory of Dec Page.

THE MAN himself knocks on my door exactly an hour later, just as he said he would.

And, yet again, he's topless.

How surprising.

He's making it very difficult not to rip down his pants right now and have him right there in the doorway. My thoughts are full of lust for the man.

I am worried our awkward conversation from this morning will carry over, but when I open the door, he flashes me a white smile and I know that he's willing to move past it.

Good.

"Hey," he says.

Stay calm, Ellie. Stay natural. Cool.

"Hi. Ready to start on the house?" I ask.

"Yeah, about that," he replies. "I was actually thinking of doing something different this morning."

I fold my arms. "Oh, really? Like what?"

He thumbs over his shoulder towards the ocean. "I was first going to take Brandy in for a swim in the sea. You want to join?"

Is this something to break the ice?

Well, screw it. Maybe it will be good for us to cool down.

I nod. "Sure, I'll tag along."

His smile returns. "Great. You get changed into swimwear and I'll be waiting at the beach."

"Give me a minute."

I get changed upstairs. I get into my bikini, feeling exposed to this man who's only kissed me an hour earlier, but I brave it.

Dec is already at the shoreline when I join him. Brandy is splashing around in the surf. When she sees me, she comes bounding over at full stride, excited. I freeze to the spot, terrified.

She stops in front of us and vigorously shakes off her water. I am doused in it. I let out an embarrassing scream and Dec laughs.

"See, how many times do I have to say that she really likes you?"

I start to laugh as well.

Fine. He's got me there.

"Yeah, yeah. She's kinda cute."

Brandy rushes back into the water and I follow her in. I think she really does like me. She jumps and plays as I slowly make my way into the freezing water. It's so cold I cross my arms and start to shiver. I turn back at Dec and he's laughing at me.

"Having fun there?" he calls out.

"Yeah, so funny," I shout back. "Mock the city girl getting into the water."

"How can I not? It's really enjoyable to watch," he replies.

I roll my eyes at him and continue in. Before I can react, a giant wave quickly forms and crashes over me. I don't have any time to get away. I'm right in the crash zone.

I'm completely soaked by the wave. Saltwater is in my eyes. I gasp for air when the wave passes. My body is freezing and all I want to do is to be back in a warm bed.

Brandy is leaping in the air, barking. Back on the shore, Dec is nearly doubled over in the sand, unable to control his laughter.

I sprint back to the safety of the beach, my arms wrapped around my body to keep me warm and my teeth chattering from the cold like crazy.

"You alright?" he asks, still giggling at my misfortune.

"Yeah, so funny," I say to Dec. "Laugh it up, dirtbag."

His face is red.

"Sorry, I can't help it," he replies. "You are hilarious, Ellie. I've never seen someone so inept in the water before."

"Yeah, yeah," I reply. I laughed as well. Even I have to admit I'm pretty pathetic with the ocean. "Well, maybe you should come to Chicago sometime and try riding the subway at rush hour, then we'll see you in my element for once."

"Come on, get back in the surf. I need to have another laugh today."

"Nope. Never."

"This is better than the movies."

I shake my head at him. "Well, now you can repay me for all this entertainment by doing up this damn house."

He flashes me another smile. "Yes, ma'am."

Maybe I was wrong, maybe things won't be so awkward between us now.

But as I head back up to the house, quickly glancing back at Dec following me with Brandy, I catch a glimpse of his solid abs and muscular frame striding across the sand, and something inside me stirs.

Yeah, Ellie. What are you getting yourself into?

How am I going to resist this man?

17

ELLIE

I can't stop thinking about the kiss.

More than a whole day has passed, a whole day of Dec and I working together on the beach house without any issues or any sexual tension, but I still can't get the touch of his lips on mine out of my head.

I think about the kiss when I paint the outside of the house. Dec leaning in close towards me as we lie in bed clouds my mind with every stroke of my paintbrush. The way I think of how he pressed into me under the bedsheets makes me blush even now.

The confidence he had to fly in close and raise his lips to mine.

The tenderness of his touch as he traced his finger up and down my body under the sheets.

Yesterday, on our first day on the project, Dec went around the house, checking it all out. Measuring things with a tape measure. He looked like a pro as he did so, a pen behind his ear. So cool and collected. So *Dec*.

He still wasn't wearing a shirt, but hey, that's also so Dec. I've come to realize it's his trademark style.

And I ain't complaining.

I watched him with deep satisfaction as he sized up the house yesterday. I like the way he works. That quiet drive of his. The way his eyes scan over everything in careful consideration, not missing a single thing. He's in his element when determining what to do about the house. A man at work. A man doing his job well is an *incredibly* sexy thing to witness.

Jen was right, he really must be the best in town at this. No wonder he's had all the girls going *ga-ga* for him over the years.

I had to stop myself multiple times from devouring him.

That was yesterday. Today he's back to work on the sink, making sure that it's all fixed. He delegated me outside to work on painting the front of the house. I hate that I can't watch him work. I feel like he's put me out here just for something for me to do, but I would happily just sit in the kitchen and stare at his perfect ass all day instead.

Yep, that kiss yesterday is driving me mad.

It was mad of me to refuse his advances, but it was the right thing to do.

The sun is glaring down on me as I paint outside. It's hot. Too hot. I check the time on my phone. Midday.

Time for a break.

I wander indoors and head straight for the kitchen. Just as I expect, Dec's cute ass is in the air as he burrows under the sink.

Yummy.

I clear my throat to get his attention. He pulls himself out.

"It's lunchtime," I say. "And I'm building up a sweat. I'm going to pour myself a glass of juice if you'd like some."

Dec wipes his brow. Like me, he is also drenched in his

own sweat. God, he looks so sexy like that. It's like he's all oiled up. His muscles bulge. He's so goddamn *manly*.

"Perfect. Thanks. A little break will do me good," he replies.

I smile and open the fridge, trying desperately to not just stare at the man's exposed torso. It's a pretty difficult task.

I pour us both a glass.

"Cheers," Dec says with a wink, clinking our glasses.

He gulps it down in one.

I see the drops of sweat drip down the sides of his neck. His wet square jaw shines in the light.

He's gorgeous.

It's just a shame that I can't have him.

He drinks it all and smiles at me.

"Was that good?" I ask.

"Very," he replies. "Nice and sweet."

"How's the sink?"

"Well, she isn't leaking anymore, so that's a pretty big success."

"Right."

"I'll probably need another hour or so work on her, though."

My pocket vibrates with an incoming call.

I shrug at Dec. "Sorry."

"No, answer it."

I take my phone out of my pocket.

The name flashes up.

And my heart sinks.

Rich Turner.

I feel the air rush out of my lungs, but I try to remain composed in front of Dec. I don't want him to see how much this affects me. I don't want him to see how surprised and shocked I am by this unexpected phone call.

I might as well talk to the guy; I've put off talking to my ex-husband for over a week now. The sooner I can sign these damn divorce papers and get rid of him from my life, the better.

If only I didn't have to talk to him.

"I should take this," I say, my voice quivering.

My neighbor just nods. He hasn't seen the name. He thinks everything's fine, but inside, all my alarm bells are ringing.

I take the vibrating phone into the bathroom and firmly shut the door so that there's absolutely zero chance Dec can hear the call.

I swipe on Rich's name and ready myself.

"Rich," I say, attempting to be cool and professional.

"Ellie? Oh, hey. I didn't expect you to pick up."

"Well, I did."

Just remember, he's on the other side of the country. He's not here. He can't hurt you anymore.

"I didn't think I'll actually get through to you," he says.

"Well, here I am. What do you want, Rich?"

Stay strong. Stay strong. Stay strong.

It would be silly to break down right here, right now.

"You got my email the other day?"

"Yep."

There's a long pause on the other end. "Damn," Rich eventually says. "I regret sending that."

"Why?"

There's another long pause. "I made a mistake, Ellie."

"What?"

"Can I be blunt with you?" he asks.

"You can be whoever you want to be, Rich. It's a free country."

"I moved too fast. I acted without thinking."

"What are you saying, Rich?"

I hear him taking in a deep breath.

"I shouldn't have asked you for a divorce," he says.

What.

Now it's my turn to pause.

I can't believe it.

"What do you mean?" I ask, my voice shaking. I can't hide it anymore.

"Um, I want you back, Ellie. I need you back."

"What are you saying, Rich?"

"Yeah, that whole divorce thing is – *was* - a mistake. This is going to sound crazy, but I've had a complete rethink over the last few days, and I think you and I should get back together. What do you say?"

What do I say?

"You've had a rethink?" I ask, stammering.

"I have."

I really can't believe it. "Now you think about it? What about thinking about it *before* our anniversary dinner? What about thinking about it before you uttered those words to me?"

"I know this sounds so stupid. I know that. I wouldn't be making this phone call if I haven't already realized how truly insane this must sound, but I need you, Ellie. I've been an idiot. I made a mistake."

"Literally a couple of days ago, you told me *in public* that you want a divorce. That isn't a minor thing, Rich. I can't brush it off like it's nothing. I can't change my mind about something like this over a phone call."

"I know."

"Well, you can at least apologize."

"Look," he says. "Let's not get emotional about this."

He's not going to apologize, I know that. I know him. Rich Turner is too proud of a man to apologize.

"I'm not getting emotional," I reply, my voice flat.

"I knew your first instinct would be to get angry at me," my ex-husband replies. "I understand that. It's perfectly sensible for you to be angry at me, but maybe you should think about it for a few days. Like I have. Go over it in your head."

"I'm not going over anything."

"You wouldn't at least consider it? I know how you operate, Ellie. I know you might need time to think this through. Properly. Logically. I'm ready to give you time, if you want, to sit on this."

"Sit on it?"

"Hopefully, you can come around to see that it's the right thing to do. I'm just here, on the other side of the phone, telling you that I want us to try again. Yeah? Let's make this work again."

I let out a long sigh. He's got me there. I do like to think things over, no matter how illogical and insane they might first appear. I pride myself on my ability to see the big picture without emotion. But I'm not being taken for a wild ride again with Rich. He had his chance, and he blew it.

"Goodbye, Rich."

He's about to say something else, but I hang up before I hear his voice again.

I grip the phone tight between my fingers. I look up into the bathroom mirror at my own reflection. I'm shaking. I'm on the edge of breaking down.

What a rollercoaster that phone call was. I can't even begin to think straight.

I stare at myself in the mirror for a long time, staring deep into my eyes until I'm steady again.

My mind is totally blank.

It's full of clarity.

I know what to do.

That was, quite literally, a wake-up call.

I know I have to do what I want now. There's no waiting around. If there's anything I've learned in the last few days, it's that life moves fast.

I leave my phone by the bathroom sink and march on right out of there, right back into the kitchen. Dec is still standing where he was, drying himself with a towel.

He looks up at me as I storm in.

"You okay?" he tries to ask, but he can't even complete his question before I rush right up to him, wrap my arms around his shoulders, and start kissing him passionately.

You know what I'm doing?

I'm doing what I want.

And it's been a long time coming.

18

ELLIE

"Are we really doing this?" Dec asks, breaking off from our kiss.

I look up at him, at his handsome, chiseled face staring back down from me. His lips are parted in such a cute way that I just want him to shut up and kiss me again.

"Yes."

That awful phone call with Rich made me realize what I truly want, and that is only one thing. Dec. There's no point in denying my feelings anymore, no point in pretending that he doesn't matter. No point in telling myself that I can't have him.

I just have to face up to the fact that I've hopelessly fallen for the surfer boy next door.

"If this is real, and I'm not dreaming," Dec whispers into my ear. "Then let me say one thing. Let me say that I want you. So much."

"You can have me," I eagerly whisper back.

"I've not stopped thinking about you for one single moment since we first kissed."

I laugh. "Me too. I've not been able to get your sexy ass out of my head for the last twenty-four hours."

It's time for me to let down my defenses. My suit of armor is completely and utterly stripped from me. I'm no longer the snob from Chicago. The successful marketing manager from the big city.

I'm now just a girl hungry for this man.

Dec can have me. Any way he likes.

"Should we go someplace better?" he asks with a twinkle in his eye.

I raise an eyebrow. "Where are you suggesting?"

"You know where I mean."

His eyes flicker upstairs.

Oh, I know exactly where he means. My bed.

I blush. "You can't seriously be suggesting this, Declan Page."

He smiles conspiratorially. "Why not?"

"We shouldn't do this."

"Why?"

"I was married a week ago."

"So?"

"This is naughty," I reply. "I'll feel like a bad girl."

"Maybe you know what it feels like. You may be all stiff and proper, but *me*? I like to break the rules. Maybe, Ellie, maybe you should know what it feels like to be a bad girl once in a while."

"And you think you're the man to make me feel like that?" I tease.

"Oh, I *know* I am."

Before I can reply, he grabs my hand and starts to lead me upstairs to my bedroom.

Oh, he's eager. I mean, I can easily tell he is by the erection that he's hiding very unsuccessfully in his pants.

I don't resist, though. I stick to him like cement, wanting to be as close to his body as possible as we navigate up the stairs.

It feels so dangerous to be doing this. So taboo.

We were never meant to be together, but now that we are, I can't get enough of the man. I'm supposed to be happily married on the other side of the country right now, not in the arms of a bare-chested surfer boy.

But I love it.

The forbidden aspect of all of this turns me on.

I bite my lower lip. Excitement tremors through my body. Anticipation of what's to come. Desire rocks my core.

I want you. That's what he said.

And I want him.

All thoughts of Rich Turner and that phone call evaporate out of my mind as I focus on the sexy, sweaty man pulling me into my bedroom. His strength surrounds me. I watch his bicep curl as he takes me towards the bed. The shape of the muscle thrills me as he hauls me up the stairs.

He's so powerful. He flings me around like I weigh nothing.

And I am gagging to kiss him. To taste his cock.

Before we fall down on the bed, Dec swings me into him. I giggle, unable to control the raging fire within me. He raises my hand to his mouth and sucks on my fingers individually. He does each finger slowly. Carefully. Savoring me.

I gasp.

My other hand runs over his exposed torso, feeling the deep lines of his wet, firm muscles. He is warm to my touch. His body is dirty from the work and dripping with sweat, but that only makes me want him more.

"I guess you deserve an award for fixing the sink," I mutter seductively.

"I do, especially if that award is *you*," he replies, and my heart flutters.

He shouldn't be in here, in my bedroom. I promised myself I wouldn't let him in here.

Well, that's all gone to hell, hasn't it?

But now that he is here, I just want to rip off his pants and let him have his way with me.

"A handsome man in my room?" I ask. "Whatever shall I do to you?"

"*Handsome*? I like that. And what are you going to do to me?" Dec winks as he pulls me in towards him even closer so that our faces are nearly touching. "I am trespassing, you know. You need to do something about that."

He leans forward to kiss me, but I push away cheekily.

He doesn't like that.

But I like to tease.

I like to see the uncontrollable desire for me burn in his eyes.

Oh, he really does want me.

"Trespassing like you did the other day when I first arrived?"

He lifts his hands and grabs my head. I guess that's code for me to shut up.

And then he kisses me.

I give in this time. I melt into him, into his overwhelming and all-consuming lust.

He's so boyish, and yet he is a man. Full of passion, but also a body of immovable stone.

I pull back from the kiss and study his face. That solid jaw. Those thick lips.

We stare at each other, and I feel the same tension

between us as in yesterday in bed before we kissed for the first time.

That tension makes my heart stop.

"I know you've wanted me to kiss you from the moment we met," Dec says.

"But it was so hard. You're my neighbor. My handyman. I told myself before I came here that I wasn't after boys."

"Well, that's before you met me," he replies.

Damn. He's so right.

And only then, when I get a close-up measure of this beautiful man's face, do I let him fuck me.

"Have me," I whisper. And he does.

In one powerful move, he turns me over and forces me headfirst into the mattress. I squeal with pleasure as he manhandles me. He's delicate and firm at the same time. A man that knows what he wants and is prepared to use his power to get it.

I am hysterical, trapped in my own desire for him. I bury my face in the bedsheets, submitting myself to him.

His hands are all over me. Pulling me out of the old shirt I've been using to paint in, ripping down my shorts. My ass is exposed to him. I wriggle it playfully in the air towards him, inviting him.

He groans at that.

"You like?" I ask, breathless.

"Hm."

He can't even articulate a proper word in the affirmative.

I like how I'm able to do this to him.

His hands squeeze my ass. I pant.

He reaches under and caresses my breasts, rubbing my nipples between his fingers. I moan loudly at his touch. He's turning me on so much.

It's good we're alone on this empty beach. No one can hear me cry out in ecstasy.

His soft touch travels down the length of my body until he reaches my sex. He plays with me. Feeling me. Making me squirm. He pushes into me. I feel his thick cock press against my ass.

My breathing shallows. I close my eyes. I feel him everywhere, as if he surrounds me. His hands work pleasure on my wet pussy. I shiver as he strokes my sex.

I feel his lips kiss my thighs. He's soft. It's like he worships me.

And then he slips two fingers inside me as I hear his jeans being unzipped.

He plays inside me, curling his fingers. My ass shakes. I feel his cock stiffen even more.

I can't stand this any longer. I just have to have him.

"Get inside me," I say, practically begging at this point.

"Oh, but I like touching you like this," he replies.

"It's... too much. I need you to fuck me. Now."

"No."

I squirm. *"Please."*

"You got a condom?"

Say no more.

I reach above me for my bedside drawer. I always have spare condoms with me, even though I didn't even intend on meeting a man here, I'm always prepared. I throw a packet at him.

"I want you inside me now," I order. "Don't you dare play around. Inside me. Right now."

He leans in close and pins both my arms down with his hands around my wrists.

"No one tells me what to do," he replies.

But he does do what I tell him.

He fucks me.

One hand lets go of my wrist and I hear him roll the condom over his cock.

But then that hand travels up again and is pinning me back down.

My eyes roll back into my head as I feel him enter me. He grunts.

And then he's completely inside.

Deep inside.

And, even more than before, I feel him everywhere. He fills me up with his cock.

His face is next to mine. He nibbles at my ear and at my neck. His hands run through my hair.

We are one.

Our bodies move together. It's like music. Like a rhythm. I just *feel* him.

We fit perfectly together.

The surfer dude and the uptight city girl.

I'm loud, and so is he. Animalistic grunts escape our mouths.

"I can't hold on any longer, Ellie," he says.

"Cum for me, Dec. Cum for me."

At my command, he does.

And then it's over.

My orgasm hits its peak. My back arches.

And he collapses on top of me.

I close my eyes and bask in the aftermath of the best sex I've ever had.

* * *

THE AFTERNOON TURNS INTO EVENING, and we don't move from the bed.

We fall asleep in each other's arms as the sun sets. Both exhausted, but in the best way possible. It's like we gave each other all of us, and now there's nothing left to give.

I enter into a deep sleep. Full of dreams.

I wake up a few hours later, at midnight.

It's dark.

And warm.

My insides glow.

"That was amazing," I whisper, expecting him to say the same words back.

But he doesn't speak.

I reach for his arm around me, but he isn't there.

I sit up in bed with the sudden realization.

He's gone.

19

ELLIE

I'M GETTING BETTER at running on the beach. I feel stronger and faster sprinting through the soft sand. Finally, my hard work is starting to break down that week of nothing but junk food and alcohol entering my body. It's starting to feel better and better with each step.

It's morning. A whole night has passed since Dec disappeared from my bed. I haven't seen him since I woke up this morning and reached for his arm around my body. I even spent a long time before I went for the run looking at his place from my kitchen window, but there was no sign of him inside.

I wonder what he's thinking, or what he's doing. Why did he disappear? It's starting to drive me crazy. Crazy enough for me to go for a run.

I run and think of last night. My body still tingles from it. Last night was amazing.

It seems like a fantasy, but I know it was real. A fantasy can't make you feel the things I still feel, even as I run across the beach. Hands down, it was the best sex I've ever had. I can still feel his hands on me. I can still feel his sensual touch.

That's why I have to run this morning. I'm on a high.

Dec was so passionate. So loving. Rough but also tender.

Oh, god.

If only I can know why he left me last night. I needed to feel his embrace when I woke up, but he was gone like a ghost.

I lower my head down and sprint even faster. I aim to run on the harder sand at the edge of the ocean. The rolling water laps at my feet as I power down the beach. I'm panting as I speed up, but I'm loving the thrill. I need to feel the strain of exerting myself.

"Hi, Ellie."

It's Dec. He's suddenly appeared beside me, running with his top off.

I slow down in order to talk to him.

"Hello, Dec."

He's here. He isn't a ghost.

"How's your run?" he asks.

"Yeah, good. Getting faster."

He doesn't seem fazed by what happened last night. He's treating this interaction so calmly. Chilled in his surfer dude way.

I don't know what to make of it. Is he going to acknowledge his strange disappearance?

Well, he's here now. That's a start.

"How about some fun?" he asks.

I stop.

Fun?

"What do you mean?"

He nods at the ocean.

"Some fun," he continues. "You and me in there."

"Is this just for you to laugh at me again?"

He shakes his head. "No. Nothing like that."

"Because I warn you, Dec. One laugh from you and I swear I'm drowning you under the waves. No witnesses around."

I guess he isn't going to mention last night. Should I?

"How about I take you surfing?" he asks.

I nearly choke.

What did he say?

"Surfing? No way."

"Oh, come on. You went swimming with me. What are you worried about?"

"Yeah, that was a light splash around in the water," I say. "*Surfing* is a whole other level entirely."

"It's not that much above a swim. Don't worry, I'll be there to hold your hand like a little girl."

I roll my eyes. "Shut up."

"I will be right beside you the entire time."

"Look, I've barely even swum in an ocean, let alone even *think* about trying surfing."

"Come on, Ellie. Live a little. Try out the surfer life-style. You're here, aren't you? Living on a beach. You might as well try it out. Tick it off your bucket list and all that."

I glower at him.

"I'm not going surfing, Dec. And that's final."

* * *

I PADDLE on top of Dec's board, trying my hardest to not think about how I'm so far out in deep water and therefore freak out.

He swims next to me, guiding the board with one hand as he kicks his legs in the water.

I quickly glance back at the beach. That's a mistake. The shore seems so far away. Miles and miles away. My heart rate bounces and, *yep*, I begin to freak out.

I want to go back. I want to go back.

This was a huge mistake.

I grab the sides of the board and try to breathe. It's difficult. I try to not think about the water. I try not to think about sharks. Or jellyfish. Or the endless depths of the ocean beneath me.

Oh, god.

Dec stops the board and turns to me.

"Hey, hey. You'll be fine," he says, slowly spinning the board around to face the beach. He sees the terror in my eyes. "Breathe. Just do what I told you on the beach, and it'll be fine. I've got you."

"Right."

He taught me how to stand up when we were on the shore before we swam in. We mimed it with the board on the sand.

But the open water is very different from the beach.

I can't believe I've signed up for this.

I didn't even get the chance to write a pros and cons list.

"Okay, a wave's coming," my surfer neighbor says, pushing me forward. "Go, go, go."

I don't have the chance to object, to say that *I'm not ready* for this.

Instead, I have no option but to paddle as hard as I can with the wave, just as Dec had taught me.

He lets go and disappears in the ocean behind me, but I'm freaking out too much and kicking my legs too hard to worry about him.

I feel the wave pick me up.

And then I'm shooting forward.

20

DEC

THE BELL RINGS when I open the door to Morgana Hardware, announcing my arrival.

I smile as I step into the store and see Aaron pop up from behind the counter. He gives me a big smile. I like the kid. Aaron knows how to please my sister-in-law. Only he and I have that skill.

"Hello, trouble," I say as I approach. I rub his hair. "Been a good boy?"

"Yes, sir."

"Staying out of trouble."

"Yep."

"How is she today?" I ask, nodding towards the back of the store.

"She's good."

"Not being too mean, is she?"

"Nope."

"Correct answer. Keep working hard."

Jen appears at the doorway leading into the back. She shakes her head at me. She's overheard my little interaction with Aaron.

"Well, hello stranger," she says. I shoot her a smile in return.

"Hi. How are things?"

"Good. You?"

"Never better," I reply.

"Still walking around topless, I see," Jen says.

I look down at my exposed chest. I shrug. "Why change?"

"You'll never change. That's what I like about you," Jen replies. "It's been a long time since you've last stepped in here, Declan Page. What can I do you for?"

"I hear you've been spreading gossip about me," I reply with a wink. "I've come here to sort that out. Nip it in the bud."

"What are you talking about?"

I lean over the counter towards her. "A little birdie has told me that you've been talking about me. Spilling out my past."

Jen acts like she's taken aback. It's very mocking. "You're not talking about the new girl, are you? I would never."

"I know your game, Jen. Don't play dumb with me. You like to talk."

"If you're referring to the time that I told the new girl that you're single and ready to mingle, then I deny all the charges."

"Face it, Jen. You're guilty."

"So, how *is* it going with Ellie?"

I give her a suspicious glance. "Fine."

Jen bites her lip cheekily. "You two... done the deed yet?"

I lean over and cover Aaron's ears. "Jen. Not in front of the boy."

"He's not as innocent as you think, Dec. He's on the internet half the day, he's seen, and heard, a lot worse. Probably worse things than either of you or I have seen."

Aaron grins at me. I roll my eyes.

"You're a great babysitter, Jen."

"Don't avoid the subject. So. You and Ellie. How's that going?"

"How do you know anything about what's going on between us?"

"Oh, some call it psychic abilities. I just call it intuition."

"Right. Whatever."

"So, tell me, have you two hooked up yet?"

I sigh. "You know, I came in here for some supplies, Jen, not to get a CIA-level interrogation."

"Bad luck, Dec," she replies. "You ain't leaving till I find it all out."

"I didn't know I was dealing with a real Sherlock Holmes here."

"Aaron, how about you finish your chores in the back?" Jen orders, turning to him. The boy glares at her, wanting to stay here and listen to us talk about my love life, but Jen's stare is stronger. He wanders around to the back of the store, grumbling. "You were saying, Dec?"

"She's a lovely girl, Jen."

"But? I know there's a *but* coming."

"But... you know me. Things for me are different. It's complicated."

She raises an eyebrow. "You're not talking about my sister, are you?"

I shrug. "Maybe. Yeah."

"You think you can't ever be with someone else because of her?"

This is getting extremely uncomfortable. I avert my gaze from her penetrating glare. I fiddle with a pen on the counter, pretending to be nonchalant.

She's right. She's gotten straight to the crux of the problem. Jen knows me well. Too well.

"Possibly," I reply, mumbling.

"For God's sake, Dec. What do you think Kendra would say if she saw you like this? Of course she would've wanted you to move on. It's been three years."

"You can't know that. You can't know what she would've wanted."

"Don't be so stupid, Dec. I grew up with her. I know her better than anyone else, except you," Jen replies, her arms crossed in defiance. "I know what she would say with you standing there acting like such a wimp. Trust me, she would've wanted you to move on. Live your life, stop worrying about things that you can't change. That's what she would've wanted."

I gulp and take a long pause, thinking. The other evening with Ellie had been magical. Beyond anything I could've imagined. But there's been a voice in the back of my mind the entire time I was with her. The voice telling me not to forget about my wife. A voice that's telling me I may even have betrayed her by getting into bed with another woman. I know it's stupid, but that feeling is still there. Gnawing at me. That's why I've avoided speaking to Ellie about what happened between us. That's why I disappeared. That night I was so caught up in my thoughts of my wife that I felt like I had no choice but to slip out of Ellie's bed under the cover of darkness and retreat back home. I couldn't handle those thoughts anymore.

I didn't know what to do, so the next day I thought I would take her surfing. Being on a board has always helped. It's been the one thing that has helped me the most in the last three years. I thought I would share that activity with Ellie. Share with her something that's close to my heart.

And I think she liked it. I dunno. I just needed to be with her, that's all, in a way that avoided us talking about what had happened.

Maybe I'm terrified of talking to her about Kendra. About my doubts. I'm afraid of telling Ellie about that dark voice in the back of my head telling me I'm betraying my wife.

"I just don't want to feel like I'm damaging her memory, that's all," I reply to Jen. She might as well know the truth. She'll see through me if I lie, anyway.

"Look, I've met Ellie, and I know you well," she says. "You two fit together, despite how opposite you may seem on the outside. Trust me when I say that lightning in a bottle like this only comes around once in someone's life, and you've been lucky once before. You're having a second chance at something that a lot of people don't even get a first chance at. Don't throw this opportunity away, Dec."

"Okay," I say. "I'll have a think about it."

Jen scoffs at me. "A think about it? *Jesus*. I love you, Dec, but sometimes you're just impossible."

"Well, saying that I do take this opportunity... what do I do with her?"

Jen raises an eyebrow. "What do you mean, *do with her*?"

"You know. Romantic shit and all that. What do I do?"

Jen throws back her head and laughs. "Wow, it really has just been you and a dog for three years, hasn't it? God, you're such a *man* sometimes, Dec."

"Well, I've not been with a... girl for a long time."

She frowns at me like I'm a useless lump. I *feel* like a useless lump. She opens her mouth like she's about to say the most obvious thing in the entire world.

"Take her on a date, you idiot."

21

DEC

I HAND the tub of paint over to Ellie. As she takes it from me, our fingers touch. Sparks fly.

God. I'm so close to her.

So near, but so far.

If we weren't so busy working, then I would gladly scoop her up in my arms and fuck her right here on the sand in the sun.

We're working on the beach house, painting the outside walls in a cool blue color. Ellie chose the shade, picking it out at Jen's store.

"You know what? I think the blue actually fits," I say to Ellie as I admire the color.

She smiles back at me. "Of course it does," she replies. "I picked it out."

"It's very... *beachy.*"

She laughs. "Beachy? Well, that's the idea."

"You've got a real eye for this stuff."

Yeah, the blue works. It makes the house look vibrant.

We've spent the whole day close together, helping each other paint the outside of her place.

But we still haven't talked about what we did the other night.

It hangs over us like a cloud. An erotically charged cloud. Okay, so the metaphor doesn't really work, but the memories of the other night are always there.

I remember how sweet her lips tasted. How soft she was. How she responded to my touch.

My cock twitches in my pants.

Not now.

That had truly been one of the best nights I've had in years.

And now I'm so awkward I can't even talk about it.

Surely, she can sense the sexual tension between us, can't she? I try to hide it all day, but it's getting hard. Even harder the longer I spend with her. Hardening every moment in her presence, just like my cock.

Everything I do with her has some kind of sexual undertones for me. Every touch as we paint. Every glance into each other's eyes when we look over. The way my focus always seems to shift on to her plump lips when she talks to me.

Let's face it, I can't get naked Ellie out of my head.

But I'm going to remain professional here and do the job I'm getting paid to do.

But that's not going to stop me from asking her out.

I think back to what Jen told me in her store.

Take her on a date.

Now, that's terrifying.

I'm still so conflicted about it, though. I mean, what would Kendra think? Would she really want me to do this? I know Jen says that my wife would've wanted this for me, but I don't know. I still have the gnawing feeling that I'm betraying my wife by falling for this girl.

I mean, I would've wanted Kendra to move on if it was me in that crash.

But... I still don't know. I feel like I'm hurting her somehow, that by lusting after Ellie, I'm erasing the time Kendra and I spent together.

I've spent years in pain. Years in mourning. Years trying to get over something horrific. I thought nothing would go right for me again. I was resigned to that fact.

And then Ellie came along, and despite my best intentions I find her face dominating my thoughts when I'm awake and my dreams when I'm asleep.

I *like* her – I know that - and there's nothing I can do to stop it.

But I've not been on a date since my wife's accident. I don't know what to do with Ellie. I don't know where to take a girl. What do they want?

What do women even expect from a date?

I've just got to face up to the fact that I'm such a neanderthal.

I've become so accustomed to living on my own, to only having Brandy as company, that I simply don't know how to treat a girl to a good night.

And that's making me nervous.

Me.

The chilled surfer guy.

Ellie has me weak at the knees.

She ignores our touch as she takes the paint off me. She's much better at hiding this sexual awkwardness than I am.

"Mind handing me that brush as well?" she asks, nodding at the one next to my foot.

"Yeah, sure." I bend down and pick up the brush she's

gesturing at. Ellie stares at the wall, biting her lip and scrutinizing it. She's good at this whole design thing. I can only fix sinks and nail wood whilst she can do this big picture stuff. She's so goddamn smart. It's driving me nuts.

She's busy evaluating this beach house and processing all the careful plans on how to fix it up and yet all I'm thinking of is how to ask her on a date. A city girl like this has *taste*, so I know I can't fail. I better know what I'm doing; I wouldn't want to disappoint her.

Here's your chance, Dec. Don't screw it.

"Um, Ellie."

She turns her head from the paint to me, staring at my eyes with her own deep brown ones. My cock twitches again under my shorts. Her face sends me crazy. "Yeah?"

"I was wondering..."

"Is it the paint? It's too lightly colored, isn't it? I've been thinking about that too. Damn, I should've bought a darker shade from Jen. I'll talk to her tomorrow."

I gently grab her wrist to quiet her. "It's not about the paint. Like I said, that blue actually works."

"Then what is it?" Her eyes go wide. I bet she's thinking of what else is wrong with the house. I like how she wants to please me.

I just want to curl up and run away.

This is, by far, the scariest thing I've done in a long time.

Just do it, you doofus. Ask her out.

"I was wondering what you're doing tonight?"

She laughs. "Well, I'm going to try to sleep without a fan."

I shake my head. "No, before that. This evening."

"I dunno. Finish this, then dinner and some wine, I think."

She's still not getting it.

"Would you like to go... out with me?"

"What, tonight?"

"Yeah. Tonight," I say.

"You and me?"

"Yeah."

"Like on a *date*?"

"Um. Yeah."

There's a long pause. I just want to die.

"Oh, sure."

"Yeah?"

She nods casually. "Yes."

My heart still doesn't stop racing.

"Great." I let out a sigh of relief.

"That would be nice."

"Good."

Okay. This feels right.

See? That wasn't as hard as you thought it'd be, you idiot.

"But, Dec," she hesitates. "Where are we going?"

22

ELLIE

"Why did you bring me here?" I ask my neighbor as I sit down at the table. I don't mean it as an accusation or anything malicious, but the words just come out of my mouth like that.

Dec narrows his eyes. "What's wrong with the place?" he asks, dejected.

He's nervous. I think that my question has freaked him out.

I glance around the room, at the customers peering over their drinks, at the bowls of nuts and the smell of beer. The last time I was here I completely embarrassed myself. I don't want to relieve that experience ever again.

"It's just that it's Blue Haven's bar, that's all," I reply.

"Well, it's the best place in town," Dec replies, taking his seat opposite mine. He doesn't seem to realize the hollowness of that statement.

I laugh. "It's the *only* place in town."

"I recall you having a lot of fun here the other night, Ellie. Don't trash talk the place."

I shake my head. "Don't you dare remind me of the other night."

"Oh, I'm never going to forget it, Ellie. You. Drunk. The way you sang, Boy, it was hilarious."

"Okay, okay."

"It'll be fun if you got that drunk again, I'm just saying."

I point a finger at him. "I am never getting that drunk again. Never ever. Not in a million years."

"Sure, you say so," Dec replies, smiling. He nods towards the bar. "How about I get you a drink?"

"Oh, don't think I don't see what you're doing here."

"I'm not doing anything," he replies cheekily. "What do you want?"

I glower at him, but I relent.

"Wine. White."

"A glass of white wine coming your way."

Dec stands up and heads to the bar.

I watch him as he sidles up to the bartender, chatting freely with the man.

I was so excited when Dec asked me out tonight. I was starting to think he wouldn't, he's been so quiet the last few days. I was worried something had happened between us and I've missed it. We haven't even spoken about the other night properly. The evening we shared in bed together, and him disappearing like that.

Instead, he took me out surfing. And yeah, it was fun. Maybe it was his way of telling me something. I still don't know what, though.

Men can be difficult animals to read sometimes, and Dec worst of all.

I think I've got to give him time. Let him emerge out of his shell when he wants to. I don't know what it must be like losing the love of your life, but I'm pretty sure it must really raise your defenses up. I've just got to slowly chip away at the wall he's built up around his heart.

But whatever's going on with him, one thing is for certain.

I am falling for the man.

I look around the bar. It's pretty busy, just like the other night. I guess it is usually packed out, being the only watering hole in Blue Haven. The same people I remember from my time on the karaoke fill the room. I'm feeling paranoid, but no one is staring over at me. No one actually cares that I made a drunk idiot of myself the other night.

My neighbor returns with our drinks.

"No shots of vodka?" I ask him, giggling.

"Not just yet, but you wait. I'm going to get you smashed."

"I don't think so."

We cheer.

I want to ask him about the other night, but I fear it'll make things awkward. I want to know why he disappeared. Was it me? Did I hurt him in some way? But, if I did, why would he be asking me out tonight? I'm so confused.

Maybe I should just ride this out and see where the night takes us. Who knows, it might be easier talking to him when we're a few drinks in.

I take a sip of wine and try to calm my raging mind.

"Hello, you two."

Both Dec and I look up to see Jen standing over us.

"Hi, Jen." Dec doesn't seem excited to see her, and she knows that, and she's grinning.

"Hey."

"You two look like you're getting along," she says, pointing between us both conspiratorially.

I raise my wine glass. "As long as he keeps buying me drinks then yes, we are getting along."

Jen raises her eyebrows at me.

"How's the beach house going?" she asks.

"Yeah, really well," I reply. "Dec's been great. We've started painting the outside."

"Is that blue dark enough?"

"It looks great so far."

"And how's tonight going?" Jen asks Dec. He shies away from her, his face red with embarrassment. He really doesn't want her to be here. It's hilarious.

"Fine."

"You look like you're having fun."

"Yep."

"You're being pretty quiet, Dec."

"Get lost, Jen."

She laughs. "Okay, that's enough teasing from me. You guys have a nice time, I'll leave you to it. Don't get too drunk, and don't do anything I wouldn't do."

She turns away from our table towards the bar, quickly giving Dec a pretty obvious wink. He sinks in his seat and groans.

"Jen's hilarious," I say, and Dec groans again.

"She's always known how to annoy me."

"I think it's probably one of her best traits."

He waves an accusatory finger towards me. "Don't you start."

"Well, since you decided to bring me to this bar as a date..."

"What's wrong with coming here?" Dec exclaims.

I shrug. "There's nothing wrong. It's just not the... *first* place I would have in mind for a date."

"No?"

"It kinda isn't."

Dec sighs and shakes his head. "Look, I've tried my best."

Bless him, he looks like a little lost puppy.

I hold his hand. "No, it's a lovely gesture, Dec. Don't get me wrong, but maybe a dive bar like this isn't the best place for a first date. Maybe it's something for you to remember for the future."

His eyes light up. "So, there's going to be a future date?"

"Don't get your hopes up. We've still only just got our drinks. The night's still young, and either one of us has yet to embarrass ourselves."

"Okay. Fine. Wrong call with the location. I get it."

"Well, you can make up for it," I reply. "If you do something for me."

"Make up for it? How?"

"Let me think."

"Oh, so you're really saying this," Dec laughs. "What do you want? What'll make us even?"

"Hm."

What would make us even?

I take a sip of my wine, glancing around the bar. I catch Jen sitting at a table with a friend.

What can I do to embarrass my neighbor?

And then my eyes land on it. The microphone.

Perfect.

Now, that's an idea.

I turn back to Dec. "You gotta try karaoke tonight," I say, my voice brimming with newfound excitement.

He glares at me, catching on to what I'm asking of him. "No, Ellie. Don't you dare."

"Sing it. Go on."

"No."

"With me?"

He crosses his arms defiantly. "Absolutely no way. I do not sing. No chance in hell."

"You have to do it," I squeal. "As repayment for thinking this bar would be a good place to take a date."

"Nope."

I'm on this now, and I ain't backing down.

This would be so fun.

"One song," I command. "Sing it with me."

Dec just scowls at me.

"No. Fucking. Way."

23

DEC

I AM SINGING.

I am actually having to sing karaoke.

Absolutely fucking great.

The awful, familiar opening chords of Journey's *Don't Stop Believing* start to play over the loudspeakers in the bar - Ellie's choice, by the way - and I start to feel the stress in my throat. Nerves. I grip the microphone in my hands even tighter and wish to God for all this to be over. I wish this is just some bad dream I'm going to wake up from.

I turn to Ellie. She's standing next to me, the other microphone in her hands. And she's grinning at me.

Oh, she's loving this. Of course she would be.

Serves me right for bringing her to this bar.

I understand now that maybe Blue Haven's crappy dive bar probably wasn't the best place to impress a girl on a first proper date. But, hey, I'm pretty rusty at this whole *dating* thing. I deserve a break.

I certainly don't deserve to be forced to stand in front of the entire town and sing some cringy eighties power ballad.

I reach for my beer. I need it. The glass is half-full. I gulp the rest of it down in one go. Dutch courage.

The opening bars of the song fade out, and now it's time to sing.

I gulp.

All I can taste in my dry throat is the bitterness of beer and the saltiness of my sweat.

Ellie starts first.

Just a small town girl, livin' in a lonely world.

She's good. Actually good.

I've not sung in years, probably not since I was a kid. I've never had a singing lesson in my entire life.

So, I already know that this is going to be pretty goddamn horrific.

I look at Ellie as she loses herself in the verse.

She took the midnight train goin' anywhere.

Oh, god. Now it's my turn.

Here we go.

Just a city boy.

Sounds are actually coming out of my mouth. Horrible sounds.

Ellie is beaming at me.

The entire bar is quiet, staring at me.

Everyone I've ever known is watching me humiliate myself, and it's all because of a girl I fancy.

I have no choice but to keep going. In for a penny, in for a pound. I can't wimp out of this now. I've just gotta get this over with. Put me out of my misery.

Born and raised in South Detroit.

Okay, no one is screaming at my singing. No one is trying to run out of the bar with their ears bleeding. Not as bad as I'd thought.

And Ellie is still smiling.

I don't even need the lyrics. I know the words from hearing this played incessantly on the car radio growing up.

He took the midnight train goin' anywhere.

You know what?

This is kinda fun.

Ellie and I sing our way into the chorus, and even though it's probably the cheesiest song in human history, I find myself really getting into it.

Don't. Stop. Believin'.

This is actually genuinely great. I close my eyes and lose myself in this song.

It feels good.

Hold on to that feelin'.

I blare out the words, loving how free I can be. This ain't half-bad. I'm enjoying myself here.

There's a flash. I open my eyes to see Ellie standing in front of me, a Polaroid camera raised in her hands.

Oh. She took a photo of me?

But I don't really care, I'm too lost in the song.

I keep going, spit flying from my mouth. I feel my shirt begin to soak in my sweat, but I don't care.

I'm actually singing.

We get to the end of the song. Everyone cheers at my efforts.

You know what? I wasn't too bad at that.

As I take a bow, I overhear Jen talking to Ellie.

"You're the first person to get him to sing."

I eye my sister-in-law. She winks back at me. Oh, I bet she loved that. Typical Jen to wind me up like that.

"Here," Ellie hands me the Polaroid she took as I jump away from the microphone. I slip it into my pocket.

"Thanks," I mumble. I've gone all shy now after my performance.

Pete the bartender slaps me playfully on the back. "Well done there, Dec," he says. "If you get a record deal, then I'll be your agent. I want twenty percent of your cut, seeing as you owe me about a hundred beers on your tab."

I roll my eyes at him and laugh.

I feel a hand take mine. Ellie's hand.

"Come on, superstar," she whispers to me in my ear. "Let's get drunk."

* * *

OH, and we do get drunk. Really drunk. We're both practically at the same level Ellie was at the other night.

And eventually we stumble home in the dark, holding onto each other for balance. We're too unsafe to drive, and maybe a walk home might sober us up.

"See, that wasn't such a bad date place," I say to the girl under my arm.

"Alright. I agree," she replies. "You were funny."

"I was funny? Don't forget, you were also up there holding a microphone as well."

"Yeah, but you should've seen how you sang. You're a natural, Dec."

"*Ugh.*"

"Seriously, you should go to Hollywood. Become a Rockstar. Get all the bling. The cars. The mansion."

"No freaking way."

"Get in a boy band. I'm sure all the girls will love screaming your name at concerts. *DEC! DEC!*" Ellie cups her hand over her mouth and yells my name at the top of her voice into the darkness.

We both laugh. The night air is chill. My back is sweaty from all the stress of that performance, but walking home like this, with my arm around Ellie, is such a happy moment.

And I know how rare and fleeting these kinds of moments are. I wish I could bottle it up somehow and keep it with me forever.

We stumble down the road. Palm trees sway over us. The road is quiet, there's isn't any traffic and we're the only people who live out this way.

We walk in quiet for some time, the only sound our breathing. The walk is sobering us up a little.

"Tell me about Kendra," Ellie whispers after a while.

My body freezes when I hear that name.

I've never really spoken about my wife to anyone before, except for Jen. But I've never unloaded my heart to someone else.

But I trust Ellie.

"What do you want to know?" I ask, breathless.

I've been so avoidant the last few days since we were in bed together. I owe her an explanation, or at least a glimpse into my heart. She deserves that.

"What was she like?" Ellie asks. I can hear the curiosity in her voice. She wants me to unload on her. She wants to hear about my past.

I pause for a long time, remembering those golden years I spent with my wife. Memories I thought I would never experience again. That was until I met Ellie, and everything shifted.

As Jen said, love like this only comes once in people's lives. I'm lucky to have another opportunity, and she's right here under my arm.

"She was beautiful," I say. And I realize it's the first time I've referred to Kendra in the past tense.

"Yeah?"

"She was my soulmate," I say. Tears start to well in my eyes. "I've been so lost without her."

Ellie places her hand over my heart.

"She must've been someone really special," she says.

"She was."

"I would've liked to meet her."

I laugh softly at that thought. "I think you two would've been good friends. She would've loved to have seen what you can do with karaoke."

"She sounds like she was an amazing person."

"Yep."

Ellie leans in closer towards me. I feel her hair on my neck. It's comforting.

"What I've come to realize in the last week," Ellie replies slowly. "Is that you can be upset that it's gone, or you can be happy that you experienced it in the first place."

That properly stops me.

"I think you're right," I say.

Ellie nods. "Why don't you tell me about her?"

She really does want to listen.

"What do you want to know?" I ask.

"Everything. Tell me everything."

And I do. Drunk, on that dark road on the way home, I tell Ellie about Kendra. About how we met in high school. About how we got married young. About how we lived at the beach house together. About how she died in that car crash. About how I scattered her ashes on that cliff.

I tell Ellie all the things I've never told anyone before. And she listens, she *really* listens to me.

And then she tells me about her life. About her husband, about her pain. And that's when it's my turn to listen.

We make our way home, telling each other our lives and we don't hold back.

24

DEC

WE BURST through the front door to my beach house, laughing and tearing at our clothes. I push Ellie against the wall, kissing her like a hungry lion uncaged, and she kisses me back equally ferociously.

She rips feverishly at my shirt. I lift it over my head.

"Mm, that's better," she coos as she sees my torso, running her hands over my abs. Even though her hands are cold, I like her touch on my skin. I shiver, and my cock hardens.

We've just come back in from our drunk karaoke session. Our walk morphed from talking about our lives to a passionate kiss on the side of the road. A kiss that turned into a hunger to fuck each other's brains out. We rushed back to mine; our bodies filled with the anxious excitement of sex.

"You want to see more?" I ask as she fingers my muscles.

Ellie nods eagerly. "Yep."

"Well, not until I see those tits of yours."

Without waiting for her response, I pull her top over her head and unbutton her skirt. She pants as I rip her clothes off.

I savagely undo her bra and moan at the sight of her hard nipples. I grab them, making Ellie moan herself. I bend down and taste her breasts. Her hands run through my messy hair. I flick my tongue over her erect nipples, feeling her squirm against me. I hold her in place against the wall.

And then I push her further up against the wall. I stand back up and bite at her neck as my hand reaches down to her warm pussy. I *need* to feel her. To feel how wet she is for me.

I play with her sex as Ellie gasps. I insert my fingers into her pussy and watch her mouth open in delight. I kiss her soft lips and bite like a playful puppy.

"Oh, Declan."

I like how she gasps my name into my ear.

"You want me?" I whisper.

"Yes."

"You want me to fuck you?"

"Yes, Dec. I want you to fuck me."

I penetrate her even further with my fingers, playing inside her as her hands tightly grip my shoulders. She feels so hot and wet. I love it. I push her even further up the wall. She stands on just her toes, balancing all her weight on me.

Then I pull out. Ellie moans in frustration.

I tear open a condom packet from my wallet.

Realizing what I'm about to do, Ellie purrs like a kitten. "Fuck me now, please," she commands me.

And I do.

I like it when she commands me. When she's begging for me.

I keep her pinned against the wall as I wrap the condom over my erect cock.

"Put it in me," she squeals.

"Yeah?"

"Yes, please."

With one powerful push, I slide into her. Her pussy welcomes me eagerly. I kiss Ellie as I thrust deep inside her, both of us still standing. She shudders, and then she lifts her legs to wrap around my waist. I take her full weight and lean her against the wall as I continue to fuck her.

She holds onto me for dear life as I thrust and thrust. I want to dig deep inside her. I want to make her scream.

And I do.

I feel her hot breath on my neck as we both come to boiling point.

"I'm going to cum," I whisper to her.

"I want you to. I'm going to."

I push up one final time inside her, my cock twitching and spluttering out with cum. She empties me completely. All I think is of her soft wet lips and the taste of her pussy as I cum inside her.

"I'm all yours," she says in my ear as I grunt. "I'm all yours, Dec."

* * *

WE BOTH WAKE up at the same time the next morning.

Ellie spent the night wrapped around me in my bed. We were unable to separate from each other all through the night. We were so exhausted from the karaoke, then the drunk walk home, and then the sex that we just fell asleep the minute our heads hit the pillow.

"Good morning," I say as we lie across from each other.

"Morning," Ellie replies. She smiles at me from her pillow, and it melts my heart. "How are you feeling?"

"Fine. Better that you're next to me."

"Me too."

"Come here," I say, lifting my arm up for her to snuggle in close. We kiss. I taste myself on her lips.

"You remember singing last night?" she asks me softly.

I groan. "Ugh. Please don't bring that up. Don't ever bring that up again."

She laughs. "I'll never forget last night," she says.

"What? The karaoke or the sex."

"Oh, definitely the karaoke," Ellie replies with a giggle. "Although the sex wasn't too bad."

"It wasn't too bad?"

"Maybe I need to try it again before I make my mind up."

"You naughty girl."

She kisses me again. "Last night was amazing though, Dec. Thank you for the date."

I hear my stomach rumble.

"You want something to eat?" I ask.

"Yes, please. I'm starving. And my body aches, thanks to you."

"You like it, though? You like what I can do to you?"

"Oh, I love it."

I lift my arm up and pull myself out of bed.

"Come on. Let's eat."

We head downstairs and I make her breakfast. Eggs and bacon and sausages. All the good things.

Ellie spends the time sitting on a stool, resting her head on my kitchen counter, watching me as I cook.

"I'm going to make you dinner tonight," she says as I plate up the food.

"Oh, are you?" I ask, my eyebrows raised.

"Well, you've made me breakfast twice already. I might as well return the favor."

I nod. "Alright. Dinner tonight it is."

It'll be interesting to see what she cooks up for us.

Ellie checks me up and down.

"As long as you're gonna wear a shirt and not just your bare chest," she says.

I shrug. I can live with that, especially if I'm getting a free meal. "Deal."

25

ELLIE

Okay, I've realized I don't know how to make a curry.

I'm no chef, alright? I don't really cook. Before I came to Blue Haven, my diet mostly consisted of pre-packed special meals prepared by my personal trainer. I barely ever did any cooking beyond warming something up in the oven or microwave. I was too busy with work and exercise to even worry about what I consumed; it was all about achieving my protein goals for the day and not necessarily about taste.

And that's how I've come to find myself having to Google how to make a spicy curry dish. I don't even know why I told Dec I was going to make him dinner tonight, seeing him standing there in the kitchen, being all sexy as he made me breakfast, just made me have to feel like I have to somehow pay him back in return.

I scroll through the different recipes on offer until I find one that doesn't seem too difficult to make.

Bingo.

I message Dec.

Okay with spicy stuff for dinner tonight?

He messages me back pretty quickly.

Love spicy foods.

Okay, spicy chicken curry for two. Coming right up.

I drive into town with the list of things to buy on my phone. I head straight to the grocery store, all ready. I ask the assistant for help, and soon my basket is full of the right ingredients.

On the drive back home, I even let myself feel a semblance of relief. This doesn't seem so bad after all. I might even be able to make something *delicious*. I just gotta follow the online recipe.

A large portion of the outside of the house has been repainted by Dec and me. A pang of pride fills me when I drive past.

Maybe everything is coming together. Maybe everything is starting to look up for me, especially after the last few nights with Dec. We've been inseparable.

Maybe we're actually falling for each other.

I did not plan on coming here, to the other side of the country, and finding love.

But maybe that's exactly what's happening.

Once home, I start making the meal, following what it says on my phone. Dec's due to come round in an hour, and Google says it should take around that long.

Perfect.

I read through the recipe one more time. It isn't hard, but I do make one change. I do dump in extra dried chilis. Dec did say he loves spicy food, so why not? I measure it up with just my eyes.

I might actually be pretty good at this. I think.

It smells good, that's for sure. I just want to impress him. I want to make the effort for him. He opened up to me last night. He let me into his heart. He told me all about his life, so making him dinner is the least I can do to repay him for that. I know opening up was hard for him to do, and I want to show him I'm grateful. That I care for him.

With the curry cooking, I get ready for Dec. He said he was going to put on a shirt for once which, in Dec's terms, is practically formal wear. I take out a nice blue dress I've brought over from Chicago. It's my favorite. It's *really* good at showing off my cleavage, and that's exactly what I want him to be focused on.

Just as I finish getting ready, there's a knock on my door.

Excellent timing.

"Hello, Ellie."

"Come in."

Dec saunters on through.

I wink at him. "Wearing a shirt for once?"

He looks down and proudly shows it off. It's a little crinkled, but I forgive him. I bet he hasn't used an iron for a long time. "Only the best for you," he says.

I laugh. "Come, let's have a drink before dinner's ready."

"It smells nice already."

"Thanks."

I open up a wine bottle and give him a glass. We chink them together and sit outside on my patio, looking out over the ocean and the clear blue sky. It's going to be dark in an hour, so we've captured that beautiful golden hour.

"What an evening," I say as I bring the wine glass to my lips.

"Yeah, it sure is beautiful."

"I can see why you live here," I reply, smiling at the ocean.

Dec nods. "It's a good life."

"But there's not much money in it."

I put the wine glass down on the table and lean back in my chair.

"I make enough," Dec replies. "Plus, I don't need much to live like this. I think some people are too tied up with materialistic things to truly realize the beauty of the world around them. I reckon sometimes people just need to stop and smell the roses in life. You don't need much to be happy."

"Well, that is a nice sentiment," I reply. "But not everyone is like that."

Dec turns to me and blinks. "What do you mean?"

"Like me, for example. I need work to keep me occupied."

"Well, there's plenty of work to be found in a town like Blue Haven. Take your beach house, for instance. That's good, honest work."

"No, it's not the same as the kind of work I was doing in Chicago."

"Oh, because you're in a big city, then somehow the work is more important?"

"It's not exactly that."

"Work here can be as equally important and is sometimes even more fulfilling. You don't need to be some higher-up in a firm sucking the CEO's dick to feel like you're doing good work."

"Is that a dig at me?" I ask.

Is he talking about Rich somehow?

Dec shakes his head. "No, it isn't."

"Okay, good."

I don't believe him. I sense a hidden bit of malice behind his tone. I think he doesn't like me questioning the little money to be made out here.

But I know I'm right.

"I'm just saying that sometimes people like to knock a

lifestyle like this, but you've seen how great it can be first hand."

"Sure," I reply. I take another long sip of the wine. The alcohol is making me feel slightly light-headed, although I don't exactly know if that's the wine or Dec's slight jabs at me. "So, you're the town's handyman? How's that business going?"

Dec shrugs. "Yeah. It's not too bad. Everyone around Blue Haven is my customer. Everyone knows who to contact when something goes wrong, especially a sink."

I laugh. "Thank you again for helping me out with this."

"It's my pleasure."

I lean forward. "But maybe you can monetize your business better."

"What do you mean?"

"Well, I am in marketing. I think I can offer up a good strategy for you going forward."

"Going forward?"

"You know, gain new clients. Maximize your workflow. Outsource. Retrain."

"Sounds like a lot of business mumbo jumbo to me. I've never been one for things like that."

"Really? Because I think you could make a big buck around here. You're the best handyman for miles around."

"Well, thank you."

"But you really could make a lot of money, you know," I say.

"Money doesn't interest me."

I wave my hand. "Of course it does."

"No, it doesn't."

"Why aren't you willing to invest in your business?" I ask. I don't believe anyone can't be interested in making more dough with their talents.

"I'm happy to live on just enough to get by. As long as I

can pay for Brandy's dog food and still have some food for me then I'm more than happy."

"But is that really what you want, though? You can easily expand. Build a proper business. There's so much potential in what you do. You could even hire out a couple of guys, make your business bigger."

"I'm happy where I am."

"But listen to me. You can start with just some basic marketing tactics. A business card. A phone number. Some advertising."

"It all sounds too complicated. I'm happy with just me."

"I can help you. I've got the skills."

"I don't want to do it."

"But why not?" I ask again. "You could be making so much money."

Can't he see that? Can't he see I'm trying to help him?

"I said I don't need the money."

Dec's face is getting red. I think he's getting a bit pissed off with my questions. He clearly doesn't like me giving him some good advice.

"What's wrong with having more money?" I ask.

"Nothing."

He's being so passive-aggressive.

"Dec, I don't like your attitude tonight. You're attacking me."

"You don't like my attitude? What about yours? You're the one trying to push me into doing something I don't want to do."

"I'm just trying to make a helpful suggestion, that's all."

"Well, I clearly don't want it."

"Okay, fine. I won't help you expand your business and make more money."

I can't help but make that passive-aggressive remark, but once the words leave my lips, I know I've spoken out of line.

"Fine."

I don't know what's gone wrong. There's tension in the air between us, and not the good kind. We've devolved into this weird passive-aggressive argument.

I don't like it.

"I'll check on the curry," I say.

Dec doesn't reply. He turns away from me and stares out over the ocean.

I go back into the kitchen, sighing deeply.

This is so hard. Why is it so hard tonight? We've been so good for the last few days.

Maybe we are different people. Too different. Maybe now our differences are finally catching up to our fantasy of being together.

I check on the curry. It looks, and smells, done. Maybe I've put too many chilis in it, I don't know.

I dish it up with rice and take the two plates outside.

Dec takes it from me without a word. I sit opposite him.

I guess we're still on awkward terms, then.

"Bon appetite," I say, trying to lighten the mood.

"Thanks," he grumbles in reply.

And I watch him pick up a fork and take a bite.

26

ELLIE

EVEN THOUGH HE doesn't want to admit it, I can see that Dec's mouth is burning up.

And it's all because of my food.

Oh, God. It's too spicy.

I haven't taken a bite yet. I swirl my fork in the curry. It looks like there's a lot of chilis in there. Yep. A lot. I drop my fork.

I'm not going to eat that.

I must've put too many in it. I've overdone the spice factor.

Dec is trying hard not to seem affected, but I can see his eyes watering and the sweat building on his forehead. He definitely finds it too hot.

He also drops his fork.

What have I done?

"Is it too spicy?" I ask.

"No. It's okay." He says it with such strain that I know something's wrong. All our strange little passive-aggressiveness flies out the window as I realize how painful my food is for Dec.

"It's definitely too spicy."

He shakes his head. "I don't want to make a fuss about this."

"No, there's no need to act all manly," I reply. "I'll get you a glass of water."

I get up to head to the kitchen, but Dec grabs my wrist.

"Please, sit down. It's okay."

His cheeks are red. Water is leaking from his eyes. The man is insane for trying to act that everything's fine. He's trying so hard to pretend he's alright, just for me.

I've screwed up big time. Serves me right for being so cocky about my cooking.

"You need water," I reply. I pull my hand free from his grasp and I make my way indoors.

"No, Ellie." Dec tries one more time to stop me, but it's too late.

I rush to the kitchen sink and pour him a glass from the tap. There's a gurgling sound from the pipes.

Oh no. I know what that means.

I look down into the basin. What's greeting me there is my worst nightmare.

The sink is overfilling.

Shit.

"Um. Dec?" I call.

He comes in, his hand over his mouth to ease the hot chilis.

"What?"

He sees the sink and I don't need to say anything. He rolls his eyes.

I understand his frustration. He's both burning up in his mouth *and* he has to fix this thing before it overflows on the floor.

First the weird passive-aggressive argument and now this? Tonight is not going well.

Dec grabs the glass of water in my hand and gulps it down, trying to cool his throat. Then he quietly takes off his shirt, gives it to me, and dives down under the sink. Luckily, his toolbox is still in the kitchen from earlier. I pass it down to him, and he gets to work.

I stand, in shocked silence, as Dec fixes the sink. He doesn't say a word, and neither do I.

It takes him a few minutes, but it's done. The pipes are no longer leaking.

He pulls himself out from under the sink and I hand him back his shirt.

"I thought you said it was fixed?"

"Well, clearly it wasn't," he replies, glaring at me. He's curt.

The awkward, horrible tension is still hanging heavily between us, I see.

"Right."

He turns to look out the window. I can tell he's thinking deeply about something.

"I better get going," he says.

"You don't have to leave," I reply. "We haven't had dinner yet."

He shakes his head. "It's okay. I think I'll just go home. I need to cool my mouth."

"I can just order some kind of takeaway if you'd like?"

"I think tonight's spark has long gone, don't you think?" he asks me, but it's not like he's actually asking me. "I'm going to go. I feel like the romance is dead tonight."

And then he's leaving. Out the door. Before I can say another word.

Gone.

27

ELLIE

Dec clearly doesn't want to speak to me.

There's been no sign of him since our disastrous date at my place. No message from him, no knocking at my door.

There's just been radio silence. Awful, painful, *nothing*.

Wearing my running gear, I sit on the bottom of my stairs and cradle my head in my hands, thinking about what on earth has gone wrong.

And I want to cry.

He's avoiding me. I've come to realize that this is his way of processing his emotions. He retreats into the one place he knows is safe. Him on his own, and only when he is ready will he open up to me.

It's completely his decision, but it makes everything so difficult. So goddamn tiring.

That passive-aggressive fight the other night led to him storming out of my place, it led to this silence now between us. And there's no end in sight.

Why did we even fight in the first place?

Because you're both two very stubborn people, Ellie. That's why.

I've only seen Dec once in the last three days, and that was only when he was out surfing. But even then, he was a long way out there in the waves. I couldn't see his face.

He didn't stop and swim back to shore, even if he did see me. And I couldn't exactly go up and say hello to him when he was so far out in the ocean.

And besides, I'm not going to be the first one to make the effort to talk.

Yep. Two very stubborn people.

I feel like I've lost him, that I might really have pushed him away forever.

No work's been done on the house since the date. I've just moped around, thinking he'll come over and talk to me. But he hasn't.

And who's going to apologize first?

Not me.

We both screwed up the other night.

Ugh.

Why is this kind of thing so difficult?

And that what's led me to now stand in my hallway with my workout gear on, ready for a run. I've decided I'm going to go run past his place. Maybe I'll even see him if I do so. I need an excuse to speak to him. I *need* to speak to him before I lose my mind.

I look at myself in the hallway mirror before I set off.

"Okay. Do this, Ellie."

Dec and I are going to need to talk.

We can't stay silent forever.

I take in a deep breath, nod at my reflection, and then I leave my house and go for a run on the beach.

The sand is warm on my feet. The sky is clear. It's a beautiful day, but my stomach is tied in knots. I'm nervous about seeing him again. The last time we were together, things did not turn out well, to say the least.

I have a feeling it was all my fault but, then again, *he* was also being such a moody asshole as well. It just wasn't a good night.

The argument came out of nowhere, but I know our differences had been bubbling underneath the surface for so long. They were going to come out somehow.

Sometimes we should just suck it up and apologize, especially to the people we most care about.

I hope this isn't the end of whatever we had, because I was really starting to like it.

I reach his house. I keep running as I look inside. It's dark. He isn't home. No Brandy is there to sprint out and greet me.

My heart drops.

I guess I won't be seeing him today. It's going to be another empty day.

I sigh.

And then I keep on running.

28

DEC

I HOPE she isn't home. I really, really hope she isn't.

I raise my hand and knock on the door. My insides churn with nerves. It was stupid for me to come over here. I shouldn't have come. There's still time for me to turn around now and leave.

I really, really hope she isn't home.

But the door opens before I can change my mind, and Jen is there. She blinks at the sight of me. She obviously doesn't expect me to have turned up at her front door.

"Hi, Jen," I greet gently. Apologetically.

She looks at me up and down. "Dec?"

"You're surprised to see me?"

"Well, of course I am," she replies. "You never come to my home."

I shrug and dig my hands deep into my pockets.

"I'm here now. Hello."

She stares at me for a long time. A little too intensely. Jen knows me too well. She can see the doubt and worry etched on my face without me even needing to tell her something's wrong.

She eventually nods at me. "Don't hang around out here. Come on in, then."

Jen lives in a small place. Like me, she's happy living on her own and she has never truly needed someone else. Sure, there's been some men float in and out of her life, but I think she prefers her own company.

The house is pretty sparse. She doesn't have much in terms of material possessions. She clearly doesn't even spend much time here at home. She practically lives at her hardware store. This house is just a place for her to sleep and eat.

I walk in and stand awkwardly in her living room.

I really never come here, but I guess today is a day I do a lot of things I don't do. I've even decided to wear a shirt today.

Jen, annoyed by my standing about, gestures for me to sit on her couch.

"Coffee?" she asks.

"Yeah, please."

She disappears into the kitchen and I sit and admire the few photos she has hanging on the wall. My eyes quickly focus on one I recognize. Taken during Kendra and my wedding. It's of the three of us, all embracing. The sun's setting behind us. We're all smiles.

That day was one of the happiest days of my life.

Even thinking about it brings a tear to my eye.

Damn, I'm crying at Jen's.

I hastily wipe it away by the time she re-enters the room. I don't think she's noticed, though Jen does have a laser-like vision. I'm sure she has and is just refusing to acknowledge it. She gives me a steaming cup of coffee and sits in her chair opposite me.

"How are things?" she asks.

I shrug. "Yeah. Good."

"Come on, there's more to it than that. Why else have you come here?"

"A guy can't visit his sister-in-law on a whim?" I laugh.

My attempt at humor does not go down well. Jen pauses. I know she's seeing right through me.

"How are you and Ellie?" she asks.

Oh, she's very good.

I shift awkwardly on the couch. "That's actually why I came here to see you today."

She sips her coffee and smiles. "I thought that might be why. What's happened?"

"I don't know."

She gives me one of her world-infamous stares. "Care to elaborate? I'm sure there's more to it than that."

I sigh. "Things were going well. And then we got into some weird argument..."

"What about?"

"It was something stupid. It doesn't matter."

"Well, it clearly wasn't stupid if it made you come around here."

I take in a deep breath. I haven't even touched my coffee yet. Ellie was the reason I came around today. After that date the other night, I've been lost in a haze of my own thoughts. Everything just came to the surface between us that night. It made me doubt everything that we had together. She's from one world and I'm from another. If we can't get over the fact that we were completely opposite people, then what chance would there be for a relationship between us? It all just felt like a lot of work to reconcile our differences, so I went back to the one thing I do know. Being on my own. I couldn't face Ellie. I couldn't put myself through the pain and heartbreak of talking to her, of her telling me it's over.

I can't face losing her. I've already lost one love.

I'm worried she just looks down at me, that she just wants to leave this town and go back to her old life the minute this beach house is done.

She spoke down to me the other night. I could tell she regards my lifestyle as below her standards. I've had enough people over the years try to change me. I've never needed their help. I don't need hers. I just want to be seen as a potential partner, not as another broken thing like a beach house to be fixed up.

I'm worried that I'm disposable, that I'm just some surfer dude she slept with as a rebound to get over her ex-husband. I'm just a handyman to help her mend this place, and then she'll be on her merry way back to Chicago. She's above me in every way, and I'm worried she'll discover that. Discover that she's made a mistake fooling around with some beach bum like me. And then she'll be gone.

It's better for me to just close up my heart, to minimize the oncoming and inevitable pain.

"She wants me to expand what I'm doing around town," I say to Jen. "She wants me to make my handyman thing into some kind of business. Get clients. Make it all *official*."

"Well, that isn't you at all."

"No, it really isn't. That's what I tried to tell her."

"You tried to tell her that? And so you two had a fight over that?"

"Yep."

Jen shakes her head. "Come on, Dec. You sure that you didn't play a role in any of this? I know you and your stubborn little head of yours. Are you sure that you didn't inflame things?"

I lean back. Always Jen to reach right into the heart of the matter. "Okay, I might have."

"So, what was the argument really about?"

"Well, it was kind of about what I said. We fought about what I should do as a handyman, and it was also kind of about our... differences."

"Right," Jen replies.

"You know, we're very different people."

"You're the small-town boy and she's the big city gal. I get it."

"Yeah, something like that."

"I see," she replies. Jen takes a long sip of her drink, thinking deeply. "You want to know what I think?"

"What?" I ask.

"I think you should stop sulking around my place and start talking to her."

"Jen..."

She raises a hand, cutting me off. "I know it will be hard talking to her. Letting someone new into your life will always bring differences. You're stubborn, that's something you both share, but that's something you both just have to overcome. If this is meant to be, then it will happen despite any superficial differences you might have. You both suit each other. Come on, admit it. You two just fit. Just shut up and go talk to her."

I let out another sigh.

"You're probably right."

"I usually am."

Jen eyes me as she takes another sip of coffee.

"How's the store?" I ask.

"Fine."

"How's everything else?"

"Fine."

"You're not going to talk to me properly until I talk to Ellie, right?"

Jen smacks her lips together. "Correct."

"Right."

"So, are you going to talk to her?" she asks.

I sigh one more time.

"I'll think about it."

29

ELLIE

I'm making lunch.

And I can't get Declan Page out of my head.

I growl at myself and continue stirring the pasta. With Dec out of the picture - and therefore practically zero work done on the house over the last few days - I've needed to put all my time on something else to fill the void. Something useful.

And who'd ever guess it would be cooking?

After that disaster the other night, I've realized I've needed to work on my cooking skills.

I've been spending my time watching cooking tutorials about Italian food on YouTube and reading up on all the various ways to fry an egg. I've watched about twenty episodes of Kitchen Nightmares in a row and have even started watching that Great British Bake Off Show. I came out here to redo a beach house, but now it seems like I'll be leaving as a qualified chef.

And I am going to leave. Well, that's what I've been

thinking of doing, anyway. I still don't know when I'm going to go but, whatever happens, I can't mope around here anymore.

Maybe I just need to shoot on out of here. Maybe it was wrong for me to think that somehow, with my willpower perhaps, I could fix up this place.

No, I'm a city girl by heart.

But who am I kidding? There's only one reason I want out of here.

And that's Dec.

He's clearly not interested in me. He's practically disappeared. I've not seen him since that time I spotted him surfing.

Should I stay or should I go?

I lean over the pasta. The water is bubbling away nicely.

And then my phone rings.

MOM.

"Hi," I say as I pick up. It's good to hear her voice.

"Hi, sweetie. How's it going?"

I blow out the air between my cheeks. "Fine."

There's a long pause as Mom assesses the meaning behind that word.

"What's wrong?"

Damn. She really knows me, doesn't she?

"It's, uh... Never mind."

I don't want to get into the full Dec situation now.

"What is it, sweetie? I know something's bothering you. You can tell me, you know."

And then I'm unexpectedly choking up with emotion. I start to sob. It's completely unplanned. Completely out of nowhere. Completely out of character.

I'm crying?

"I think I've made a mistake," I say through the tears. "A big mistake."

"What do you mean?" Mom asks.

The sobbing comes thick and fast. Tears fall from the edge of my cheeks into my pasta. I'm practically unable to squeeze the words out coherently.

"I just want my old life back."

"What's wrong?"

"It's... there's a guy I've met."

"A guy?"

"But we've fallen out, and I think it's for real this time."

"You think he's gone?"

"Yep."

"Forever?"

"Yes."

"Oh, sweetie. You've had your heart broken twice in a matter of weeks. You're not okay."

"I'm fine, Mom. Really, I'm fine."

"Well, forget about the beach house. Maybe you should come home."

"I said I'm fine."

"No, you aren't. I can hear it in your voice."

I wipe away my tears. I really don't want to get into this now. I'm too fragile. "I am fine. Don't worry about me."

"Is there anything I can do?"

"I'm about to leave to meet a friend," I lie down the phone. I need to cry in peace. I don't want my mother to hear me sob. "I've got to go."

"You can always talk to me, Ellie."

"Bye, Mom."

I hang up and spend a few minutes leaning over the sink, crying.

I just miss Dec.

I miss what we could've shared together.

But it now seems like it's all gone.

I strain out the pasta. It takes double the time, because

I'm still choked up from the crying on the call with Mom, but I'm so hungry.

I sit down on the balcony outside and eat, watching the waves roll in and out, and my crying slows.

Maybe I should think about leaving. I should listen to my gut. If one phone call from Mom can break me down like that then maybe I should just get out of here.

I've nearly finished the bowl of pasta when my phone rings again. I pick it up and answer, thinking it's Mom calling again. I can probably talk to her with more calmness this time.

"Hey."

Just imagine my shock when it's Rich's voice that answers.

"Hello, Ellie."

Not him. Not now.

"Rich? Why are you calling?"

"Ellie, I need to talk to you." His voice is soft and nervous.

What does he want?

"Look, Rich. I can't have a conversation like last time. You can't ask for a divorce and then ask me back, like, a week later."

"I made a mistake, Ellie. I need to talk to you about it."

Even though he's on the other side of the country and unable to see me, I raise my hand as if to stop him. "It wasn't *just* a mistake, Rich. It was life-altering."

"What can I say, Ellie? I want you back."

"I... can't."

"Why not?"

"I just can't."

"Have you thought about it?"

"Yes, and it isn't going to happen."

"Please, Ellie."

"Goodbye, Rich."

I hang up before he can utter another word. I have heard enough. He can't keep calling me back like this.

Not now.

It's because I'm worried I'm so fragile I might actually relent to him. I'm worried I might actually crawl back to Chicago. Back to him.

Honestly, anything is better than me moping around here.

The man wants me back, and now I'm seriously considering it. If he does actually apologize, if he does actually seem like he's changed for the better, then I might as well follow up with his pleading. I'm not cut out to live out here. I should be back home. With a single phone call back to Rich, I can be on a plane in a few hours back to the life I had. That wouldn't be so bad.

But then I would never see Dec again. I would have to erase this week from my mind.

Damn, why is everything so complicated?

I thought coming out here would make things easier, but then I met Declan, and everything just got a hell of a lot more complicated. I really thought I was coming out here to escape my heart troubles, but it seems like I've jumped from the frying pan and into the fire.

I rub my eyes and stare out across the beach.

Dec's lights are on.

He's home. And still we haven't talked. It's been days now.

This is getting ridiculous.

Okay.

My mind's made up.

I think I will leave soon, for sure. Go back to Chicago. Maybe even go back to Rich.

But first I'm going to talk to the man opposite.

I'm not leaving until I put some kind of closure on what's happened between us.

But I'm not in the mood right now. I'm not in the mood for anything but to snuggle into bed with some book to take my mind off everything.

I will leave Blue Haven, but before I do, I *will* speak to Dec.

And I will do it tomorrow morning.

30

DEC

"Come here, Brandy," I call out.

My dog rushes up to me in response. I get down on all fours and wrap my arm around her soft, fluffy body.

"Good girl."

We start play fighting. I tickle her on her stomach, and she growls. I feel her tongue lick my face in revenge and I laugh.

I get up off her and head into the kitchen where I've got a surprise waiting for her. She eagerly follows me in.

I pull out the bone from the shopping bag.

"You want a bone?" She runs up to me, panting excitedly. "A big juicy bone?"

She barks. Oh, she wants it.

I chuck her the bone. Brandy goes ecstatic over it, chewing and biting on the thing.

That'll keep her occupied for a while.

"You're the only girl who's never given me problems," I say to her as she gnashes at the bone.

I pour myself a glass of water and look out the window at Ellie's place. I'm still thinking about Jen's conversation yesterday.

Maybe I will speak to Ellie.

I still haven't done anything about it, though. I still haven't summoned up the courage to go over there and talk to her.

I don't know why.

Maybe I'm terrified of her response. I don't want her to leave. I don't want to end what's been going on between us.

I'm scared of endings. That must be what it is. I've had one unexpected ending before, and I don't ever want to experience that again.

Sometimes it's better to close up your heart so that you don't get hurt.

I down the glass of water.

Wait...

I squint my eyes.

I see Ellie through my window. She's walking towards my place.

Yep, it's definitely her.

And she's moving fast.

Oh shit.

I dash to my front door and open it to see my neighbor coming straight towards me.

"Dec?"

"Ellie."

She stops at my doorway. This is the first time we've seen each other since that date the other night. "I was just coming over to talk to you," she says.

Right. So, she's here to apologize?

"Great," I reply. "What can I do for you?"

"We need to talk."

"Sure. About what?"

"You know what."

"I really don't."

"You've been avoiding me. I've been avoiding you."

"Okay."

She glares at me. "Don't use that tone, Dec."

"What tone?"

"It's the same tone you used the other night, all passive-aggressive."

"I'm not being passive aggressive."

"There you go again."

I roll my eyes. "What are you here to talk about, Ellie?"

"Us."

I lean one arm against the door. "What about *us*?" I ask.

"Why were you so angry the other night? So passive-aggressive?"

"So, I guess you're not really talking about us. You're instead wanting to talk about *me*. I see how it is."

"Come on, Dec."

I pause and take in a deep breath. "The other night was weird."

"It was."

"There was something about the way you spoke to me. It was like you were talking down to me. I didn't like how you were trying to push me into something I don't want to do."

"You mean your business?" she asks. I slowly nod my head. "I was just having a discussion."

"It seemed more than a discussion," I reply. "It seemed more of an attack. It seemed like you wanted to attack the way I live. Just because I don't live in some fancy skyscraper in some city doesn't make my lifestyle wrong."

"That's not it at all," Ellie says. "I wasn't trying to attack you. I was trying to offer you solutions."

"Yeah, solutions to non-existent problems. I like my life,

Ellie. I don't need you or anyone else to tell me it's wrong or what I need to do to fix it. I've had plenty of people tell me that over the years, I don't need you to. I thought we were equals, but the way you spoke to me felt like I was beneath you. I'm not something for you to fix."

"What do you want me to do?" she asks. "Apologize for trying to make your life better?"

"And now *you're* being all passive aggressive."

I don't know why I'm being like this. I think I'm just trying to put my defenses up.

Like Jen said, Ellie and I are two very stubborn people.

Maybe I think that by being all snarky that I can hide my emotions. That I don't feel the pain of the separation I know that's coming.

"What is the issue here, really?" Ellie asks, her voice strained.

I might as well tell her my fears.

I sigh. "It's been a long time before anyone has affected me like you have, Ellie. A long time. I've not let myself get as intimate with another person for years, and it actually scares me how much I've fallen for you. It *really* scares me."

I'm being so honest here.

She turns her head away to the side and pauses for a long time. When she looks back at me, I see a tear fall from her eye.

"It still doesn't give you the right to act so rudely," she says.

She still wants to attack me? After I've opened up to her?

I guess she's not who I thought she was.

"Rude? That's a bit rich."

"Yeah. Well, it's true. You have been acting rudely. Plus, you haven't even come around to fix the place in the last few days, as we had agreed. That's pretty rude. Why have you ghosted me?"

"You're going to have a go at me for that as well? Everything's my fault, yeah? What have I done right?"

"Seems like nothing in the past few days."

"Yeah, I'm the bad guy."

"Well, I'm not the one who kissed me, fucked me, and then disappeared," she replies.

I'm taken aback by that.

"I don't even know why I put up with this," I say quietly.

"Me neither."

"Good to hear."

"We're different people, Dec," Ellie says. "It seems like we want different things in life."

Here it comes.

She wants to end it all.

Why do I allow people to get so close that they can hurt me?

"Why are we different?" I ask.

"We should never have met," she replies. "If it wasn't for my divorce and then this crazy idea about fixing up the beach house, then we would never have met."

"And is that what you think? You want to end it all just because we're different people?"

Ellie groans and takes a step back. "I can't keep arguing with you like this. I'm going back home."

"Okay."

"Not there," she gestures back at the beach house. "I want you to know I'm going back home. Proper home. I'm going back to Chicago."

My heart drops, but I'm not ready to give in just because she's dropped this bombshell.

"Okay. Bye. It'll be nice to have the beach to myself again."

It hurts.

I knew it was coming, but it still hurts.

She's leaving me. Forever.

I had another chance at love, and I completely blew it.

And here it is. Another unhappy ending.

"You know, you're such an asshole," she barks at me.

"Whatever."

I hide my pain well. She has tears in her eyes, but she can't see me crumbling inside.

Ellie growls at me, turns, and marches back towards her place.

I slam the door in response, making sure it's definitely loud enough for her to hear.

I want her to think I'm angry, but in reality, I'm falling apart.

31

ELLIE

His door slams behind me.

But I continue walking.

I don't want to break down until I'm safely inside the beach house. I don't want him to have the satisfaction of seeing me cry.

What has just happened?

I didn't mean to tell Dec that I'm planning to leave Blue Haven. I was meant to healing the rift between us by marching over there and demanding to talk, but what happened instead was that I blurted out words I know I can never take back.

I'm going back home.

I open and slam my own door with a bang when I get back to my place.

Is that what I really want to do? Go back to Chicago? Never see Dec again?

Maybe I will go now.

There's nothing for me here. Not after that conversation.

I was right. We are two different people who both want different things. We are unreconcilable.

I stand in my hallway and rub the tears from my face.

"You came out here to fix up this damn place, Ellie," I say to myself. "Not to fall for a stupid man. Why are you even here?"

That's it.

I head upstairs to my bedroom. I reach under my bed for my bags.

I'm going to leave.

I start to unhook my dresses from the hangers.

I'm going to go right now. I can't stand it here anymore.

And then there is a knock downstairs. A knock on my front door.

I stop, and I tut.

Dec.

It's him. He's probably back to apologize. Or maybe even to argue some more.

I might as well go and talk to him, especially if he's made the effort to come over here.

Then I can really let him know I'm planning to go.

I head back down the stairs, taking in a deep breath.

I stop before I open the door. I remind myself it's too late for him to apologize. I'm going home, and that's final.

I pull open the door.

But it's not Dec that's standing there.

"Mom?"

She immediately wraps her arms around me in a tight hug. I know she's real by her perfume, the same perfume that I remember from my childhood.

"Oh, Ellie," she says in my ear.

"What are you doing here?" I ask her, stammering. I'm completely overwhelmed by her presence.

She hugs me even tighter. "I couldn't forget about our last phone call, and how upset you seemed, so I decided to get on a flight over here."

"You got on a *flight*?"

"Yeah."

"You flew out just because of one phone call? Mom, I said I was fine."

She pulls out of our hug, frowning at me. "Ellie, I am your mother. I can tell when you're upset over something. I'm not going to let you be upset on your own, especially not after the last few weeks you had."

"You're insane."

"Well, I am *your* mother."

I shake my head. "No matter how crazy you are, it's good to see you, Mom."

She squeezes my hand.

"Let me have a look at what you've done with the place," she says, twisting her head around to take in the beach house.

I laugh nervously. "I haven't done much, barely anything since I've arrived. In fact, I was thinking of going home. I was just packing upstairs when you knocked."

Mom blinks. "Were you?"

"Yeah. I think I'm over Blue Haven. I reckon we should just sell this place, and quickly. It was stupid of me to think I could do anything with it."

"Well, that's why I came all this way," Mom replies.

"Really? What for?"

"I've got a surprise for you."

"Oh, no. Not one of your surprises. What is it?"

"Well, after our phone call, I thought you might need

something. Then your surprise got into contact with me. Said you've been talking."

It takes me a moment to register what she's saying, but when I do, my mouth drops.

"You aren't saying what I think you're saying, Mom..."

I remember her insane ideas in the past. This surprise sounds no different.

She points behind her at the car that she's driven up in. The car door opens.

And out he steps.

"I thought you two need to talk," Mom says, but my attention is not on her. It's on the car, on the man who's just stepped out of it.

It's him. My husband. He's actually here.

Rich Turner.

32

DEC

"Come on, Brandy."

I whistle, and my dog follows me. I gesture with my hand for her to jump into my pickup truck. She does so eagerly, and I climb in after her.

I turn to her, my hands on the steering wheel. "Ready?"

She barks.

I turn on the ignition and drive away from my beach house.

We pass by Ellie's place on the way to the road. There's some car parked in front of it. I haven't seen it before.

I wonder what she's thinking inside there.

I shake my head and continue on.

With Brandy excitedly poking her head out of the window next to me to catch the cool breeze, I steer the vehicle onto the highway down the coastline.

My destination isn't far, and soon enough, we reach it. An empty stretch of beach.

I park the car by the side of the deserted road and hop

out with my dog. She runs around as I stroll away from the pickup truck. I don't even lock the doors. I know for a fact there's going to be no one around to steal it.

I walk up to the edge of the cliff overlooking the empty beach.

It's the same spot I scattered my wife's ashes.

I sit down on a patch of grass close to the edge. The wind is strong up here. I can taste the salt blowing in from off the waves.

I close my eyes, drinking it in.

My wife and I used to come here. Back when things were happy. Back before I knew what real pain and grief meant.

And now I come back here often, as a kind of pilgrimage. Despite her always in my heart, this is where I feel closest to Kendra. If she was ever going to linger some place on earth, it would be here where I scattered her ashes.

Sometimes, if I listen hard, I think I can hear her.

I take in another deep breath.

"Hello," I whisper.

The wind doesn't answer back.

I sit for a long time, just taking it all in. My mind is blank.

I try to remember Kendra. What she was like. Her smell. Her taste.

Her laugh.

I sit there in silence until I start to speak. I pretend to speak to her.

"Where to start?" I ask the air. "I have a lot to tell you, a *hell* of a lot. A lot has changed in the last week, Kendra. And it all feels like it's for the better. It really does, but it's hard. It feels so hard. Especially when you're not here."

I sigh.

Maybe I'm crazy, talking to just the empty air like this.

"I want to tell you something, Kendra," I say. "I've met someone. Someone who I think might be perfect for me. I know an opportunity like this is so rare, but I don't know what to do. I *really* don't know what to do, Kendra. And I think I've screwed it all up. I really have. Maybe it's because I feel like I can't move on from you that I've gone and ruined what I have with this girl. I don't know. But we had a fight. It was over some stupid shit, but it's still torn us apart, and I don't know if we can be put back together."

Still no answer from the wind.

"Kendra, I feel like I need you to tell me what to do. You were always so good at giving me the right advice. I miss it. I miss you."

I take in a deep breath and continue.

"Her name's Ellie. She's beautiful and smart and *good*, and she's somehow captured my heart even with me trying to seal it off. I bet you two would've been great friends. She even laughs at my stupid jokes, just like you used to do. She's just perfect in every way, but I'm scared of somehow betraying you. I don't know. Jen says I'm being stupid. Maybe you think so too."

I shake my head at myself and open my eyes.

What a weird thing for me to be doing, asking a dead person what I need to be doing. It's just so ridiculous.

Kendra isn't here anymore. She's gone. This is just some place I scattered her ashes. I don't even really believe in an afterlife and all that religious mumbo jumbo. Why would I ever think she'll speak to me from beyond the grave?

What am I even doing here?

"What do I do?" I ask the wind and the waves and the emptiness. I must as well take one final chance. "How do I fix this? How do I tell this girl that she means everything to me when I've already ruined everything?"

I don't hear anything back.

See?

Stupid.

I pull myself up. I brush the dirt from my hands. I head back towards the pickup truck, calling Brandy to join me.

And then it hits me. I double-over by the truck. What hits me is stronger than a thought. It's clearer than a word. I can't describe it.

It's like a feeling. An idea.

But something truer. Something in both my gut and my heart.

Kendra.

It must be her.

And she's trying to tell me something.

33

ELLIE

"Look, Rich..."

Mom raises her hand to stop me from speaking any further. "Please, Ellie," she says. "Please listen to what he has to tell you before you say anything."

My eyes turn back to my ex-husband standing in my doorway.

"Can I at least come in?" he asks.

I say nothing.

"Yes, come in," Mom says, gesturing him inside.

Rich shuts the door behind him and steps into the living room. He looks around the inside of this crumbling beach house.

I just stare, dumbfounded, at him. I cannot wrap my head around him actually being here.

"You're probably wondering what I'm doing flying to the other side of the country," Rich says, a shy smile on his face.

"Yeah. A bit," I reply, arms crossed. "But I think I know why."

"Please listen to him, Ellie," Mom interjects. "Give him a chance."

"Why should I?"

"I believe he's changed. We've been speaking, and I believe he wants things to be different."

"You brought him out here?"

"I thought that you two should talk."

"Really?"

"Yeah. I know how upset you've been. He's clearly made a mistake with the whole divorce thing and maybe you should listen to him."

"You and Rich have been speaking behind my back?"

Before Mom can answer, Rich interrupts her.

"I'm sorry, Ellie."

That one sentence from Rich freezes me. I turn back to him, my hands trembling.

He's sorry?

"What?"

"I am sorry," Rich continues. "For everything. For asking you for a divorce. For freaking out like I did and breaking things off with you. I wish I could go back and reverse it all. It was all a mistake. A terrible mistake, and I'm sorry."

I honestly don't know if he's being real or not. I don't know if this is a fake performance. I really don't know what to think anymore.

"You're apologizing?" I ask him, stammering over my words.

"I haven't even signed the divorce papers yet, Ellie. Legally we're still married. We can slip right back into our old life."

"Just slip on back, right? Like nothing happened?"

"You have to admit it, we fit together, Ellie. We work together. We know each other so well. There's no point in throwing that away for the sake of your pride."

"And you're sorry?"

"I am."

"For embarrassing me like that at the restaurant? It came out of nowhere."

"What do you want me to do?" he asks. "Get down on my hands and knees and beg?"

"That would be a start."

"Ellie, you must see that it isn't right for you to keep this back anymore. We should be together. We *work* together. How many times do I have to tell you I'm sorry?"

I open my mouth to respond, but there's a knock on the door.

Who could this be?

We all turn to the sound. I look at Mom.

"I better answer that," I say.

I leave the room, ignoring Rich, and head to the front door to open it.

It's Dec. He has his hands behind his back, clearly holding something hidden from my view.

Dec is here? Can this get any crazier?

"You can't be here," I snap at him, whispering so that Mom and Rich can't hear. I don't want them to meet him. I don't want today to get even weirder.

"I'm here to talk," he replies.

"Everyone seems to want to talk to me today. Look, I want you to leave."

He doesn't move.

"No. I'm not going until you hear me out," he says.

"Leave, Dec."

"I know things have been weird between us, but I want to put that behind us."

"I want you to go."

"Ellie."

"Not now," I bark.

"Okay, okay," he replies. "I know you're upset. I'll just leave you these."

He brings his hands out from behind his back. He's holding a bunch of flowers. Yellow chrysanthemum flowers, and there's also a little note attached to their stems by a blue ribbon.

I take them from him with a scowl.

"Go, Dec."

Getting the message finally, he turns and leaves.

And I shut the door.

34

ELLIE

"What are those?" Mom asks, looking at the flowers in my hand.

I don't reply to her. I just stand by the closed door, staring at the ground. My mind is blank.

"Ellie? What are they? Are those flowers?"

He got me these. My favorite. He remembered my favorite.

I blink, brought back to reality.

"Huh? Yeah. They're flowers."

Mom nods.

I step back into the living room, still in shock at what Dec has given me. I grip the bouquet close to my chest and look around. Mom is staring at me. She knows something's up, but Rich doesn't seem to care. He's frowning, head turning from my mother to me. He seems more annoyed that we've been interrupted than about the flowers in my hands.

"Where were we before that knock?" he asks the room,

irritated. "Right. We were talking about us getting back together, weren't we?"

"Um... yes," I slowly respond. My mind is still blank.

"I was saying how compatible we are, Ellie. You should come back to Chicago with me instead of languishing in this strange old beach house. Come back to civilization."

"Go back with you?" I ask.

He rolls his eyes and checks his expensive gold watch. "Okay, I've had it. I'm not standing around here any longer arguing about the semantics. I've apologized and you've accepted. Let's just hurry on out of this stupid town and back on a jet. We can sort out all the details back in Chicago, back in civilization. Come on, you two."

Rich stamps his foot on the ground and starts to head towards the front door. My Mom looks from Rich back to me, concerned.

My ex-husband is ordering me about, but I am in no hurry. I'm still looking at my hands, at the gift Dec got me.

"What's my favorite flowers?" I ask him before he gets to the door, my voice trembling and quiet.

"What?" Rich can't hear me.

"What are my favorite flowers?"

My ex-husband stops and spins around.

"Flowers?" he asks, bewildered at what I'm asking him.

"Yeah. What are my favorite ones?"

"What a stupid thing to ask," he replies. "I don't know that. Why would I know that?"

"You don't know?" I ask.

His eyebrows furrow. He's irritated by my question. "No, I don't. Why are you asking this now? We've got a plane to catch. Let's not fuck about here another minute. Don't worry, I'll get my guys to sell off this stupid place for you. You'll never have to think about this god-awful Blue Haven town again."

"We've been together for three years, and you say that you know me so well. You say we are compatible in every way, but yet you don't know what my favorite flowers are. What are they?"

He looks flustered. "Come on, Ellie. Stop being so ridiculous. Why would I know something like that?"

"I must've told you a hundred times in the last three years."

"Well, it seems pretty irrelevant to me. Of course I wouldn't remember."

My voice is soft, but my words are sharp. "I will ask you one more time, Rich. What are my favorite flowers?"

Rich shrugs. "I don't know. *Roses*?"

He spits out the word like it's nothing.

But no, it is *everything*.

It seems like only one man in my life can remember such a tiny detail about me like what my favorite flowers are, and he's not standing in this room. Only one man loves me for *who* I am, and not for *what* I am.

Only one man doesn't want to change me. I've been a fool trying to change him.

Our differences are what make us stronger together, not divided.

Declan Page is that man.

I pause. I know the next words out of my mouth are going to be life-changing for me.

"Get out," I say.

"What?" Rich asks, mouth agape.

"Leave. Go."

He can't believe what I'm saying. I've never stood up to him like this.

"What are you saying?" he asks.

"You divorcing me was a blessing in disguise."

"Don't be so stupid," he replies. His insult just washes over me. I don't care.

"I came here. I discovered who I am. I met the love of my life. And this was all in the space of a week. I've been living a lie. Coming out here has made me realize that."

"I don't get it."

"I am not coming back to Chicago with you, Rich," I reply. "I'm staying here. Without you. Luckily, you divorcing me means I don't have to do it to you myself. We're over, Rich. We've been over for a long time."

"Ellie. If you let me go, then you're going to lose your job. You don't want that, do you?"

I don't believe this man.

He's threatening me?

"You're really resorting to that?"

"The only reason you've been promoted so high is not because of your talents or skill, but just because of me. Because of the good words I've put in. You don't have any real talent."

Because of him?

Yeah, that might be so, but I don't need him anymore. Not when I have Declan Page.

And yeah, I *do* have talent.

I raise my head to look at the man square in the eyes.

"I don't care about the stupid job. Stick it up your ass."

Rich, his face red, tries to change tack. He tries to appeal to my sensitive side. His voice goes all gentle.

"Ellie..."

But I immediately see through it.

"Go. Now."

Rich is many things, but he is not a stupid man. He can read the room. He glances at Mom. She's a stony wall in response.

He points a threatening finger at me. "This is a stupid

move you're making, Ellie."

"No, it's the best move I've ever made in my life. It's the *right* move."

He harrumphs and storms out of the house, leaving the front door open behind him. A moment later, I hear his car drive away. It skids on the sand. The city boy doesn't know how to drive out here.

And then it's all quiet. He's gone.

It's all over. My marriage. Done.

For good this time.

With Rich gone, I let out a long sigh. It's like I'm being deflated from all stress and anxiety.

He really is gone.

And I don't want to think about him ever again.

I look down at Dec's flowers in my hands. I find the note tied to them and flip it around.

I'm surprised to find that it's not even a proper note at all. Instead, it's the Polaroid I took of Dec singing karaoke.

The photo makes me instinctively smile as I remember that night. The best night of my life.

Scribbled below the picture are two words.

I'm sorry.

It's the most genuine apology I've received today.

"Ellie?" It's Mom. I haven't realized that she's been calling my name over and over. "Ellie? Are you okay?"

I turn to her. She's just witnessed all of that. No doubt she's very, very confused.

"I've changed my mind," I say to her. "I'm not going back to Chicago. I'm staying here."

"I don't understand."

"I expect you don't," I reply. "There's a lot I need to tell you - and I will - but right now I need to do something."

I rush out the front door before Mom can open her mouth.

35

DEC

Ellie's at my door.

I don't even expect it. When she told me back at her own door to go, I thought that was it. Forever. I saw the car out front. I didn't know who exactly had driven up to her house, but I had the sinking feeling that she was about to leave Blue Haven for good.

That's why I gave her the flowers it was because she was going. I wanted her to know that I am sorry.

I had realized I had lost the best thing that's happened to me for a long, long time, and it was all because I'd been a selfish idiot who didn't see the miracle in front of me before it was too late.

It's what Kendra would've wanted me to do. That's what I think I heard her saying to me back there on the edge of the cliff. She wanted me to apologize. I knew it was the right thing for me to do. It's the only thing for me to do. To show Ellie I do care.

I got Ellie her favorite flowers and resigned myself to the devastating fact that I would never see her again.

And it had been my fault.

I did not expect her to turn up at my door not soon after. I was happy to just let her know that I am sorry before she left forever.

But now she's here. Standing on my doorstep with her beautiful face looking up at me. Her cheeks are stained with tears.

"Hello," I say when I see her.

She's out of breath. It's like she's sprinted over. Like she's been in a panic.

"Hi, Dec."

"You okay? You want a glass of water or something? You look a state."

She waves me away. She breathes out and stares at me for a long time. "I'm sorry too," she says.

"Pardon?"

"The Polaroid. What you wrote. I'm sorry too. I don't know why I ever doubted us."

And then she falls into my arms, hugging me tightly. My heart is ready to burst out of its chest. I kiss her hair. She smells like the ocean. Salty and wild. I like it.

"No, I'm sorry," I reply. "I've been a massive asshole. I pushed you away because I was afraid of opening up to someone, especially someone as magical as you."

"And I tried to change you when I should've realized you're perfect the way you are," she replies, her face buried in my naked chest.

"I guess we've both been asshole," I say, and she laughs. I feel her tears wet my shoulder.

"Whose car was outside your place?" I ask.

"Ah, my ex-husband's. Well, his rental."

"Your ex-husband's? *What*?"

She grips me tighter. "It's a long story. But he's gone and now I'm here with you. That's all that counts."

"Yeah," I reply. I kiss her lovely hair again. "That's all that counts."

I am going to find out about the ex-husband. And maybe kill him for letting Ellie go. Or I might thank him.

"Oh yeah, also my Mom's here," she mumbles into my chest, her arms still wrapped around me.

"Are you keeping her waiting by being here?"

Ellie leans out of the hug. She looks at me with her wide eyes. Her smile sparkles in the sun.

"I don't care," she says before she kisses me. "She can wait. I just want to stay here with you."

"You can stay forever, Ellie."

36

TWO MONTHS LATER

ELLIE

"Let's put some music on," I say. "How about you do it, Aaron?"

The boy's face lights up. He stops playing with Brandy and instead rushes over to the speakers and my phone resting on top. The dog follows him, barking. He swipes through until some new pop song is playing.

The kid knows how to put on a good song.

"That's very loud," Mom says, raising a hand to an ear. I roll my eyes at her.

"Just have a drink and dance," I tell her, laughing.

She frowns at me.

"Did I hear *drink?*" asks Jen, emerging from the bathroom. She has a massive smile on her face.

"I think Dec's getting the drinks," I reply. "If he hurries up, that is."

"Hello, hello, hello. Did someone mention my name?"

Into the living room steps Dec. He's proudly waving a champagne bottle in the air.

"How about a toast?" he continues. "Gather round folks."

We all do. We all get into a circle in the middle of the redone living room. Aaron, Mom, Jen, Dec and me. My neighbor pours a glass for each person - and a soda for Aaron - and he raises his in the air.

"It's been a tough few months putting this place together," he says. "But with all your help, we've finally done it. Blood, sweat, tears, and all."

"That's true," I continue. "I don't think we could've done it without your store, Jen. Or you helping us, Aaron. Or your emotional support, Mom. But it's finally done."

I look around the room. I look at the beach house around us. Everyone follows my eye line. The building is completely renovated and redone. Repainted and restored. All with the help of everyone in this room. Now it's a proper house and the envy of Blue Haven.

Mom stayed with me, helping us. Jen also lent a helping hand, recruiting Aaron to be a willing apprentice.

And now we've done it, both Dec and I. Months of hard labor to get the house like this. It was an effort every single day to spend all our daylight hours on it, but it's paid off. Really well.

I've built a house, but most of all, I've built a *home*.

"Cheers," Dec says.

We all clink our glasses. Brandy barks.

I look at Jen. She smiles at me. I smile back.

My heart is so full at this moment it's ready to burst.

Congratulating ourselves, we all split up. Jen starts dancing to the music with Aaron. Mom sits down on the couch and watches, laughing.

"Let's do karaoke," Jen says, and Aaron gets very excited about that. "How about you join us, Ellie?"

"Oh, no. I'm worried about how drunk I might get if I pick up a microphone."

I slip out of there just as they start *Don't Stop Believing*. I step onto the porch, admiring the view and sipping on the Champagne. I need a moment alone to soak in the feeling of accomplishment.

We've really done it.

I watch the waves rise up in the ocean.

This is my home now. I wouldn't have it any other way.

The door opens behind me and Brandy shoots past my leg, dashing towards the sand and playing in it.

I feel an arm wrap around my waist behind me.

Dec.

"Hello, pretty lady," he says quietly into my ear, squeezing me tight. "What are you doing out here?"

"Admiring the view," I reply, resting my head back on his muscular arm.

"Yep. It sure is a nice one."

"It is."

"I was talking about the view of your ass and not about the ocean," he says before pinching my buttocks. I slap his hand away, giggling.

"Stop it, wild boy."

As well as us working on the house together, the last two months have been a total fuck fest with Dec and me. We can't get enough of each other's bodies. We spend our days fixing up the place, and then our evenings swimming and surfing in the sea, and then our nights in each other's beds.

It's been amazing.

And pretty sore for me.

We've worked through our differences. I've realized I actually *want* to stay here, and Dec has realized that maybe

I can help him. I'm going to help him launch a brand new handyman business. He'll be the talent, and I'll be handling everything behind the scenes. Marketing. Accounts. Paperwork. He won't need to do anything he doesn't want to do because I just simply *love* that stuff.

He just gets to work, and so do I. Supporting each other.

Our differences make us an unstoppable team.

And I can't wish for more.

"How about a walk?" Dec asks.

I nod.

We stroll across the beach together. Brandy darts between us, running in and out of the ocean. I watch him.

Dec and I are quiet, just walking together in a comfortable silence.

That's until he opens his mouth.

"I love you."

I turn my head away from the sunset to focus on him.

"Pardon?"

His voice is quiet but firm. "I love you, Ellie."

I reach for his hand.

"I love you too."

It's so true and so obvious that it's so easy to say. But it feels so right.

He grips my hand tight and pulls me in close.

"Come with me," he says.

Before I can ask him what he's doing, he's pulling me across the beach, all the way to behind his house. To a little alcove of beach. We're completely out of view from anyone else, from even the prying eyes from my beach house. It's just us and the sand and the roaring of the ocean.

He guides me down to the sand and falls on top of me, kissing me passionately. I kiss him back, turned on by his sudden urge for my body.

His fingers trail down my body to my waist. He teases

me with a delicate circling around my wet sex, causing my body to burn up.

God, I want him so bad. I always want him so bad.

He nibbles at my ear.

"I love you, Ellie," he repeats. I can just melt in his voice.

I am breathless and panting.

"I love you too, Declan Page."

And, before I know it, he's pulling my shorts down. I let him, my hands rushing down to unbutton them to help him. My finger brushes his fully erect cock and I gasp. I start playing with him and Dec's eyes roll back.

"I want to cum inside you," he moans.

"Then do it," I command.

He enters me.

And we fuck. Under the clear sky among the sand, with the waves crashing behind us.

Dec and I screw each other on our own little stretch of beach.

After we both climax, we don't say anything else to each other. We don't need to say anything else.

We walk back home in silence, hand in hand. Together.

EPILOGUE

ELLIE

"Why have you taken me out here?" I ask Dec as we stand on the edge of the cliff. I avoid looking down over the edge. I know it's a long drop to the beach below. I don't have to look down to know that.

He stands turned away from me, staring out over the ocean. He seems perturbed by my question.

Slowly, he twists back around to face me. He looks me in the eye. I could melt in his serious gaze.

This morning he told me to come with him. He didn't say where we were going despite my incessant questions; he just got me in his pickup truck and drove out here to this empty beach. To this cliff overlooking the ocean.

"Why are we out here?" I repeat. I still can't guess.

"To see if this is right," he replies, his voice soft.

"To see if what is right?"

Dec ignores me. Instead, he closes his eyes and takes in a deep breath. It's a long wait before he speaks again. The wind brushes my hair. I feel the salt of the ocean spray upon my cheeks.

He opens his eyes and grins at me.

"It is right. She's smiling down on this. This is the right thing to do."

Oh. I get it now.

He's talking about Kendra. I know now. This must be the place he scattered her ashes, the place he famously never takes anyone to.

Until me.

He must've been talking to her, to check with her about something. To see if something was right.

But what?

I get my answer straight away. Dec kneels down in front of me and pulls out a little box from his pocket.

A ring.

"Ellie, it *is* right," he says. "This is right. I've known you through some of the toughest times. We've built a house together. We've built a home together. There's only one thing left, only one thing left for me to give you. I've already given you my heart, but now will you marry me?"

I really have made a new home here. Dec is my home, and I'm his.

There's only one answer I can give him. The truthful answer. The right answer.

I feel the wind gently lap against me as I utter one word. "Yes."

ABOUT THE AUTHOR

Rebecca has had the storytelling bug since... forever!

What Rebecca likes most is writing steamy hot filthy romances with sweet happy endings sprinkled with some delicious bad boys.

Born and raised in an Aussie coastal town, she loves travelling around the world - meeting new people and discovering their stories.

Aside from adventuring she also enjoys a good rainy day in with a good book or at a hot beach catching the sun.

She's a world-class napping professional. You'll most likely find her asleep snuggled up on a sofa somewhere cozy.

For other titles and information please visit
rebeccacastle.com

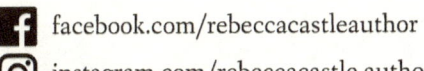

facebook.com/rebeccacastleauthor
instagram.com/rebeccacastle.author

www.ingramcontent.com/pod-product-compliance
Lightning Source LLC
Chambersburg PA
CBHW030629120726
47904CB00006B/2092